BEAST

CLARISSA WILD

Copyright © 2022 Clarissa Wild
All rights reserved.
ISBN: 9798838954985

This is a work of fiction. Names, characters, places and incidents are either the product of the author's imagination or are used fictitiously. Any resemblance to actual events, places, organizations, or person, whether living or dead, is entirely coincidental.

All rights reserved. No part of this book may be reproduced, transmitted in any form or by any means, electronic or mechanical, including photocopying, recording, or by any information storage retrieval system. Doing so would break licensing and copyright laws.

Content Warning can be found on my website: clarissawild.com/beast-tw

To all the girls who got told they weren't beautiful enough to deserve love …

Kill them with kindness.

ONE

BEAST

My world is shuttered in darkness.

Behind these bars, I become one with the shadows.

I sleep in them. Breathe in them. Live in them.

I simply just ... exist.

Until ...

CREAK.

The door at the top of the stairs opens, and a sliver of light is cast down into my cell.

Onto me.

Huddled in the corner, I stay put, eyes half-closed but vigilant.

THUD. THUD. THUD.

Two feet slowly appear, as though it costs him great trouble to even walk. Then the rest of his body reveals itself, his chest rising and falling with each step as if even coming down here costs him a great deal.

Patience.

Energy.

Everything I have.

Everything he doesn't.

I watch as his wrinkly face comes into view. His lip curls up, barely taking the time to form the word as he spews it. "Beast."

My nostrils flare at the sound of his voice. At the beckoning and my mandatory call.

But I stay put in my cell, watching him from afar.

A filthy smile appears on his face. "I have a job for you."

His hand dives into his pocket, and he pulls out a photograph of what appears to be a family of just two. A man with a potbelly and a beard just like my owner's and a girl with her back toward the camera, huddled over a piano.

My owner approaches my cell and presses the photograph against the bars. "Bring me his head."

I step out from the shadows and into the light. Every footstep is another thud on the stone ground beneath my feet. His body quakes the closer I get until my frame towers over his. Until the only thing separating us are thick metal rods.

My house.

My prison.

I snatch the photograph from his hand and study the image carefully, taking in every detail. The colors, the view behind the window, the man's wretched smile … and the girl's beautiful, flowing black hair that reminds me of the sea of shadows I call home.

A small strand of hair tucks behind her ear, and an inch of her blushed cheeks are visible, along with the edge of rose coral lips hiding behind the veil of darkness.

A hint of a smile.

Like a promise.

A secret.

I swallow.

"Kill anyone who gets in your way."

My eyes flicker up to meet his. "*Anyone?*"

"I don't care." His lips curl up like a wolf. "Kill. Them. All."

Kill.

I like that word.

It's all I've ever known.

All I've ever understood.

The only thing that will ever get me where I want to be.

Out.

Two

Aurora

"You." *PUNCH.* "Mother—" *PUNCH.* "Fucking." *PUNCH.* "LIAR!"

I open the door at the last slap and peek through the narrow gap. Downstairs, my father's raised fist makes my heart beat faster as he shakes the blood off his knuckles.

"I swear, we didn't know," the man on his knees in front of him says.

His face is bloodied and mauled.

"Disgusting." My father spits on him. "I should've known better than to trust you with this fucking shipment."

"We were ambushed!" the man replies.

WHACK!

The hit is so hard and fast that the man's whole body turns sideways, and his eyes meet mine.

I gasp and close the door for a second, calming my speeding heart.

But I can never fight the urge to look.

"I'm sorry," the man mutters as I peer downstairs again.

"You should be. Do you know what this will cost me?" my father yelps. "EVERYTHING!"

"I'll get it back," the man says. "We have the weapons. We can fight them."

"You've done enough," my father barks. "I want you out of my sight. NOW!"

The man hurriedly gets up and runs outside, leaving bloodied handprints all over the door. My father wipes the back of his hands on a napkin. Then his eyes connect with mine.

I hold my breath, close my eyes, and shut the door.

"Aurora."

Too late.

Sighing out loud, I frown, slapping my forehead. "Stupid, stupid, stupid!" I mutter to myself.

"Come here." My father's monotonous voice forces me to open the door again and take in the full brunt of his disappointment in me.

His eyes narrow when they meet mine, and I swiftly close the door behind me and walk down the stairs.

"Didn't I tell you not to eavesdrop on my business?" he

says.

I nod. "Yes, Papa. I apologize."

"Save it. I know you'll do it again."

I avert my eyes and play with my hair to ease the tension. "I just want to know what it's like."

"What what's like?"

"To run a business like yours," I reply.

He snorts and then begins to laugh so loudly my face turns red. "You think you still have a shot? After what happened the last time I involved you in my business?"

I wish I could hide, but there is no hiding from the ridicule of my father.

What happened all those years ago still haunts me.

Yet all he sees is a mistake.

"Oh, you innocent little girl." He turns and throws the napkin onto a table in the hallway. "For someone with such a way with words, you really don't understand much about this world, do you?"

My lips part, but I don't know how to react.

Suddenly, the housekeeper steps inside the hallway and stares at us.

My father clears his throat. "Never mind."

"Sir, your guests have arrived," the housekeeper says.

"Where are they?"

"I told them to wait in the foyer."

"Offer them a drink while I clean this up." My father rubs his hands and gazes up at me. "Get ready."

I nod. "Yes, Papa."

I quickly close the door again, but my heart is still going a million miles an hour. Even though I've seen him use violence so many times, I never get used to it. Not in my heart nor the many gruesome pictures floating through my mind.

Maybe that's why he doesn't want me to watch.

***

Past, age 7

"I told you not to cross me!" My father's voice booms through the living room as the door to the apartment smashes open.

BANG!

My eyes close from the loud noise, but they instantly pop open the second I hear a piercing howl.

My father's personal bodyguard shields me while my father's men step inside the apartment and hover over the man crawling across the carpet in a desperate attempt to get away.

BANG!

His movements stop. All that's left is blood pooling below his belly.

And I stare without making a sound.

Just as my father told me to do.

Watch and learn.

Maybe then you'll be useful someday.

So I force myself to watch as they pick up the man and empty his pockets until they find his phone and toss it to my father. "Let's see what that fucker's been up to."

The sound of whimpers coming from across the room draws my attention ... along with that of the men.

I suck in another breath.

They line up, guns at the ready, slowly stepping over the man's body to get closer to the bedroom door in the back.

My father presses his finger to his lips, signaling me to keep quiet.

My legs begin to tremble.

The door slams open.

A woman steps forward with a gun in her hand, roaring out loud with tears staining her eyes.

BANG!

A shriek cuts off in my own throat at the sound of her body hitting the floor.

She didn't even have time to shoot.

And I knew from the moment they heard her that she'd be dead within seconds.

Even though I've never seen her. Even though my father has never seen her.

All it takes is a single mistake by a family member, and everyone is done in my father's eyes. And the man lying in a pool of his own blood, his hands reaching for the very same door the woman just burst out of, paid with his life.

His family.

Blood for blood.

I swallow as the men swarm around the woman to check her pulse and sift through her things. It's all so surreal to me. I can barely stomach it, and once the adrenaline wears off, my stomach starts to flip over.

I run out of the guard's safe arms and head for the toilet, throwing my head inside as I empty the contents of my stomach.

The men in the other room haven't even noticed I'm gone, and I doubt they care. They're far too busy searching the apartment for evidence and stolen money. Not even my father seems to have taken notice of my absence as he cusses while rummaging about the apartment, kicking furniture to rid himself of his unkempt rage.

I sigh and flush the toilet, rinsing my mouth in the sink before tapping the towel against my lips. The very same towel that must've touched those people's faces mere hours ago.

I drop it and stare at the girl in the mirror, with her shoulder-length black hair and almond-shaped eyes, feeling like she aged years today.

Another wave of nausea overcomes me.

Until I spot two glinting eyes in the corner of the mirror staring straight back at me.

My heart stops.

Fingers clenched around the sink, I hold my breath, wondering if I'm hallucinating.

Until he blinks.

The second I move away, he does too, hiding behind the

curtain rail of the bathtub. My gaze shoots to the door, checking to see if anyone's watching before I make a move.

I step closer, heart pounding out of my chest, curiosity fueling every muscle. My brain is telling me not to do this, to go back to the living room and tell the men there's someone in here.

But my heart … My heart aches the second I carefully peel away the curtain to reveal a boy, probably the same age as I am, huddling in the corner of the tub.

Shivering.

I'm overcome with fear.

Fear of what might happen when they come inside.

Anger at the mere idea they could kill an innocent boy.

That my father could make that decision.

Instinct tells me to stay away, but my heart forces me to reach for the boy, despite my hesitation. My fear. His.

Because I can see the terror in his eyes. The hope lost with every passing second.

How do I make it go away?

He must've heard what happened out there to his mom and dad.

I pluck at my hair and take out the single pink flower my personal assistant put there when she did my hair, and I offer it to the boy as a gesture of peace.

He glares at me without saying a word.

I push it into his hand and fold it over, adding a gentle smile.

I know it's not a lot. In fact, it's not anything when

faced with death.

But I want to give him something.

Anything.

Even if it means nothing to him now.

It could mean *everything* later. When the dust has settled and all that's left is the silence of the dead ... At least there will be life in his hands.

"What's going on in there?" My father's harsh voice pulls me from my thoughts.

I yank the curtains to quickly close them again. "Nothing!"

My father peers inside. "Someone in there?"

"No, I checked. I'm on my own. I'm just sick." I cover my stomach with my hand. "Had to vomit from all the blood."

My father's face contorts at the sight of the sickness on the toilet seat. "Well, finish up. We're leaving."

I nod and wait until he's gone before I peek at the boy over my shoulder, who has remained silent all this time.

My lips part.

I don't know what to say.

Nothing I say could ever undo what just happened.

Nothing I do will ever stop my father from handling his business exactly the way he always has.

Violently.

***

Present

Papa never took it kindly that I tried to save that kid from his wrath.

Once he found out, he returned to the apartment, of course, to no avail. The kid was long gone, along with my father's patience for me.

One attempt at making a choice, and already I had all of them taken away from me just like that.

"AURORA!" My father's booming voice makes me step on my own dress.

"Fuck," I mutter, stumbling across the carpet. I really wish he wouldn't scare me like that, but nothing I say will ever make him change his mind. I learned that a long time ago.

I open the door while also putting on the straps of my heels.

"Come downstairs. The guests are here," he hisses. "You're taking way too long."

"Yes, Papa. Coming," I say, and I hurry down the stairs.

"Where are your gloves?!" he mouths. He grabs my shoulders, spins me, and pushes me back up. "Get them. Now."

Sighing, I run back upstairs on my heels, clutching my little black dress with one hand while I open the door to my bedroom with the other. I fish my favorite pair of gloves from my closet—white with a rose embroidered on top—and put them on.

I run downstairs, sliding my hands down the banister just as my father's guests enter the hallway.

"Oh, how lovely. Is that your daughter?" says a woman with puffed-up brown hair and a voluptuous body. Next to her is a suited-up man with a chiseled jaw.

But all I can stare at are her red fingernails with such intricate details that they're almost like a painting. And it makes me jealous.

"Why don't you introduce yourself, young lady?" my father says, wearing a fake smile.

"Hi, my name is Aurora Blom."

"Walter Janssen," the man says. "And my wife, Dana."

I offer them both a hand. "It's nice to meet you."

"Likewise, and so well-mannered too," Dana says, nodding at my father.

My father seems chipper at the compliment, but all it does is make my lip twitch.

If only they knew what it cost me.

I ignore the little voice in my head.

"Let's head toward the coffee room to discuss this new venture, shall we?" my father says.

The two follow him through the hallway, and we all sit in the coffee room where our housekeepers have placed three steaming hot coffees and a plate of expensive cookies filled with cream.

Everyone takes a cup, except me, because no cups are left.

For a reason.

My father doesn't like it when I drink coffee. It makes me spirited. Happy.

He doesn't like that either.

I grab a cookie and chomp it down just like my feelings.

"I heard your daughter is an excellent pianist. Is that true?" Walter asks.

"Absolutely," my father says, and it momentarily makes me smile. "Though she can definitely still learn a thing or two from her instructor."

My smile instantly vanishes.

Why do I ever think it'll be different?

"Nevertheless, I'm quite eager to hear her play," Walter says.

"She'd be happy to." My father eyes me down. "Right, Aurora?"

"Of course, Papa," I reply, putting down my half-eaten cookie on a plate and making my way to the piano. Sitting on the bench makes my heart slow as I stare at the keys. I carefully plant my fingers on them, making sure my gloves won't get caught between the keys when I start playing the notes.

Like a melody coming alive, my soul sings to the music I play, the notes pulling me apart at the seam like a string from a dress. And even as a tear begins to form in my eye, I continue to play as best as I can.

A single tear rolls down my cheeks as the song comes to an end and my fingers leave the keys. I quickly brush it away.

"Wow," Walter says, his approval making me turn and smile. "That was amazing."

"And all that with the gloves still on?" Dana says. "Darling, why don't you take them off? You must be able to play easier without them, right?"

I clutch my hands, a blush forming on my cheeks. "I, uh …"

My father's stern eyes watch over me. Threatening me.

Don't.

Not ever.

The same eyes he uses on me each time I cross his line.

Each time I destroyed my last chance at a semblance of a life outside these walls.

But I have no one to blame.

No one but myself.

"In any case, beautiful," Dana mutters.

Beautiful.

I gaze down at these hands.

These hands can bring beauty into the world.

They are anything *but* beautiful.

BANG!

Shaken, I sit up straight, eyes widened. I'm not the only one.

That almost sounded like … a bomb.

Both Dana and Walter peer down the hallway where the sound came from. "What was that?"

My father seems incensed. "I have no idea," he mutters, quickly getting up.

Two guards run through the hallway toward the front door, guns pulled and all.

BANG!

The room starts to fill with smoke.

Dana's eyes fill with horror, and she begins to scream.

I quickly get off the piano stool and crawl onto the floor. I don't know what's happening, but I know it can't be good.

"Peter, get my guns!" My father's voice echoes through the halls as he calls our best guard.

BANG! BANG! BANG!

Gunshots.

Oh God.

Coffee drops to the floor, spraying the carpet, as Walter grabs Dana's hand and runs into the hallway toward the bathroom. Within seconds, their bodies are blasted right back into the foyer with a giant hole in the middle of their chests.

My eyes widen.

It's happening. It's really happening right here in this house.
They brought my father's business right to his doorstep.

Several guards come into the room, covered in holes and bullet wounds. They stumble and fall, smearing the carpets in blood. One of them makes their way toward me before he collapses right in front of me, his arm flopping down onto my leg.

Panicked, I shove it off, nauseated by the thought of a dead man's body resting on top of mine. My heart beats in my throat as Peter runs in and hands my father his guns, and they both begin to shoot at whatever comes down the hallway.

I can barely see a thing other than the bursts of fire emanating from the guns being fired.

But the sounds—good God, the sounds—of screeching metal upon stone, lumbering footsteps like those of a giant, the splattering of flesh and blood ... those are nightmares come to life.

Within seconds, a figure in cargo pants and thick protective gear appears through the fog, barely visible but immense, towering over everyone here.

My father points his gun at the giant.

BANG!

The bullet bounces off his chest like there's metal underneath.

And it makes my entire body shiver.

The man moves lightning fast. With one quick jab, my father is on the ground, crying out in pain. There's a visible cut on his arm, oozing blood. And his gun has been kicked far away.

"No, please, don't kill me!" my father begs.

Oh God. This can't happen. Not him too.

Without a second thought, I crawl out from under the piano and slip my hand underneath the dead guard's jacket until I find his gun. I swallow away the fear and shoot without thinking.

BANG!

The strong recoil throws me back against the piano, and I instantly lose my grip on the gun.

OOMPF!

All the air is knocked from my lungs, and I collapse on the floor.

Our eyes connect as the intruder barges straight past my father. My breath hitches in my throat. Eyes like an emerald dream but with the face of a monster, he's scarred from top to bottom and wearing a thick, metal collar around his neck. He's bigger than anyone I've ever seen. Just one of his shoulders is larger than both of mine combined. And every step he makes reverberates through the ground.

THUD. THUD. THUD.

Just like my heart, he quickens his pace until he's right in front of me, staring down at me like a hellhound ready to kill anything in its sight.

His hand lowers and grabs my throat before I realize it, and he manages to lift me off the ground with ease.

"No, p-please," I gasp, unable to form a single sentence from the sheer pressure around my neck.

He lifts me to meet his gaze, eyes narrow and darkening. Until they suddenly open wide, pupils dilated.

His grip around my neck loses all force in an instant. I'm dropped to the ground, coughing loudly. "Please, stop," I mutter, tears staining my eyes as I look up.

But the figure gazes over his shoulder instead, searching for something—or someone—who is no longer there.

Father?

"Papa?" I cry out, glancing between the thick calves in front of me.

The figure's chest rumbles with a growl emanating from deep within. His head slowly turns back to me, square jaw tightened, nostrils flared, the emerald glimmer replaced by pure hatred.

He bends over and picks me up by the waist, throwing me over his shoulder like I weigh nothing. Screaming, I kick and punch, but to no avail. He carries me out of the living room, marching across the bloodied floor and over the bodies until the last whimper of the fallen pervades my home in permanent silence with the slamming of the front door.

And my life as I knew it, in all its pain and beauty, ceases to exist.

Three

Aurora

I'm thrown into a van in broad daylight. My wrists are locked in place from behind, a thick strap keeping me from freeing myself. When I scream, he grabs me and pushes a piece of cloth into my mouth. Then a bag is pulled over my head.

Darkness.

Pure and utter darkness.

Terrifying.

My nostrils flare as I breathe fast and desperate, even though the bag has holes. The panic only rises the second he closes the doors.

Silence.

Oh God.

Why me?

Where is he going to take me?

And where is my father?

I hear something unlock and hold my breath as a door opens. Someone steps inside in the front. I can hear two massive feet settle as he sits down on the chair.

The engine starts, the sound only adding to my crippling fear as the van begins to drive. My breathing is labored and noisy. I feel like I'm lost in a nightmare I can't escape. I sit up straight and try to focus on seeing through the bag, but it's impossible. All I can do is breathe through the tiny holes, in and out, in and out.

C'mon, Aurora, focus.

Listen to the sounds, feel the way the van moves, and remember the directions so you know where he's taking you.

But the longer it takes, the less I remember about the entire journey, forgetting lefts and rights everywhere until it's all one jumbled mess and makes me want to cry.

After a while, the van stops.

My heart palpitates so fast it feels like I might have a heart attack.

I stay still, cornered in the van, and when the driver's door shuts again, I jolt.

The van doors crack open.

I shriek into the cloth and scoot back on my ass as two hands grasp for my legs.

The man grabs my ankles and spins me around so I'm helpless to fight back as he drags me out of the van.

With a simple motion, he throws me over his shoulder again as though it comes naturally to him.

SQUEAK.

A door is opened.

"Look what the cat dragged in."

It sounds like a woman, but definitely not a voice I recognize.

"You look like you just stepped off a battlefield," the woman adds.

The man holding me like a victory prize merely growls at her.

"You want a room?"

The sound of money clattering onto the counter catches my attention.

"You can stay for the night, but I need you and your business gone by tomorrow, understand?" the woman says. "I don't want any trouble with the cops."

No verbal response from my captor.

THUD. THUD. THUD.

His footsteps are like moving mountains as we go up a staircase. And another one. Three in total. Then some more walking. A door opens and shuts, and I'm thrown down again onto soft bedding. My breathing is ragged as my body sinks into the mattress, and I struggle to turn my neck.

Suddenly, he swooshes me around, and I kick around wildly to get him off me. Until he rips the bag off my head, and I come face-to-face with the devil's hound himself.

But all he does is stare.

Straight into my soul.

***

BEAST

For a moment, it's as if time stands still.

There is nothing in this room.

In this world.

Nothing.

Except her … and me.

Her caramel eyes enchant me, forcing me to pause and take in her beauty. Her rage. Her tears.

Some of them tumble down her cheeks, her eyes desperately searching mine for answers. Answers I don't have.

But the moment passes, and she spits out the cloth I pushed between her lips. "What do you want from me?"

My lips smash together, and my fists tighten as she tries to slide off the bed.

"Don't move," I growl.

"What are you going to do to me?" she asks, tears staining her eyes. "Are you going to kill me?"

The question sounds so simple.

The answer should be yes.

Should.

When I stood in front of that piano, fingers locked around her throat, I thought of nothing else but choking the life out of this girl until nothing but another body was left on the pile. Just for trying to get in my way.

Until our eyes met, and I saw my own reflection through her pupils.

And for the first time in forever, I felt something more than pure and utter rage.

My fist tightens so harshly my nails dig into the palm of my hand, and I turn around and start pacing the room.

I should not be doing this.

I should not have brought her here.

I should've killed her when I had the chance.

I glance at her over my shoulder, but she keeps staring at me, making it hard to focus.

The second those eyes chose mine, I was lost.

I growl to myself and immediately turn to charge at her. She shrieks as I approach, my hands at the ready to curl around her neck again and end this swiftly. I have to. For my sake. For my owner's. For her.

No.

I stop right before the tips of my fingers hit her skin.

She whimpers. "Please, don't kill me."

I pause and stare down at my fingers, her skin. My senses come alive, prickling with energy like lightning.

She looks up at me with doe-like eyes, shuddering with

fear. "Please. There must be something I can give you. Do you want money? My family has plenty."

My nostrils flare.

She thinks I can be bribed with money? Wrong.

Her lips part. "My father can pay you what you want if you let us both live."

Her father.

I grasp her face with one hand, pressing her cheeks together, forcing her to listen. "Where is he?"

"I don't know," she replies, crying. "Please, don't hurt me."

Hurt her?

I must admit, the thought did cross my mind several times.

I almost killed her.

Almost.

But something about the way she looks at me stops me from going too far.

I lean in and lift her face so I can look into her eyes. Her face is round and puffy, lips heart-shaped and petite but pink, her neatly kept black hair all bungled up from the messy ride, but I know what it looked like before I raided that house.

She looks like a porcelain doll.

An expensive one, but a doll nonetheless.

I put her back down on the bed and continue pacing around the room to try to make sense of things.

One thing I know for sure is that I never miss my target.

Except for today.

Fuck.

Blom should've died.

I was *this* close to fucking ripping off his head.

Until I got distracted by his daughter raising a gun at me, and he escaped.

And now I'm left with her.

What the fuck do I do?

I pause and turn to look at her.

My mere gaze has her crawling back on the bed until she reaches the edge, her fingers searching for anything to grab onto, even when her wrists are tightly locked together with a strap.

What could she possibly hope to achieve?

She couldn't use anything in this room against me and win.

And I think she knows that, judging from the petrified look on her face.

"What are you going to do with me?" she asks.

Hmm …

That's right.

What *am* I going to do with her?

I can only stay in this hotel for a single night. My owner expects me back in the morning. With a head. Which I don't have.

All I have is this girl.

She's seen too much to be let go. But I can't kill her either.

"Please, I'll do anything. Just don't kill me," she murmurs, tears rolling down her cheeks.

I've seen girls cry before, but never one as pretty as her.

And never once before in my life have I felt the need to take a girl up on her offer.

Until now.

***

Aurora

Suddenly, he marches toward me, and I shriek again, "No!"

Too late. His hands are already around my ankles, dragging me down the bed until I'm flat, and he spins me around to lie on my belly. Then he crawls on top of me, his weight bearing down on me as I kick around helplessly.

"Please, I don't wanna die!" I beg.

He grasps my wrists, pinning them to my back, and pulls out a knife.

The same knife that easily sliced through my father's arm.

My mind is sinking into a hole so deep I don't know if I can crawl out of it.

This is it. This is the end.

Oh God.

I'm not ready. I want to live.

The glinting knife inches closer and closer, and I close my eyes, not wanting to see the finish line.

SNAP!

The tie wrapped between my wrists drops off.

My eyes flutter, a panicked heart reminding me my blood is still pumping through my veins. I'm still here. I'm alive. He didn't kill me.

I breathe a few ragged breaths as he slowly slides off me and tucks the knife back into his pocket. After a while, I push myself up from the bed, staring him down.

Why did he release me?

What's going on?

"Why did you …?" I can't even finish my sentence because of the way he looks at me.

His presence is as overwhelming as his size, not to mention the killer look in his eyes. I bet he could end my life before I could even blink.

Goose bumps scatter on my skin.

Did he free me because of something I said?

Because I told him I'd do anything to live?

"If you want money, I can get you what you need," I say.

I don't know how, but I can make it happen. I have my own account, and if push comes to shove, I can always call the bank and ask about my father's account.

"I don't need your money," the man growls back.

What else could he want from me? Unless …

I swallow and inch closer to the bed, ignoring the fear

settling in my heart when I look at this beast of a man. I slip closer and closer under his watchful eye, and without a second thought, I go to my knees in front of him.

His eyes narrow as my hands approach his belt slow and steadily so I don't push him into retaliation. I don't want him to see me as a threat. I don't have any weapons.

All I have is my body.

And if I can use it to stay safe, I will, even if it goes against every fiber of my being.

I pull at his belt until it comes loose loop by loop and drops to the floor. His eyes never leave mine as I open his button and pull at the zipper, which has to cross a substantial bulge. In fact, the second it's all down, I actually gulp at the size.

Am I able to do this?

What other choice do I have?

I tug at the band of his underwear, but he grabs my wrist and pulls it away from his crotch even though I was about to pull it down.

His hand slides down the smooth gloves and curls underneath the fabric. When he's about to pull it up, I tear out of his grip.

He eyes me down with disdain.

"I ... I want to keep the gloves on," I say, swallowing.

His jaw tightens as I move back to his belt, but he pushes my hand away every time I try.

Doesn't he want this?

Every man wants this, right?

If he doesn't want my money, this is all I have left to offer to save myself. So why won't he let me?

"I don't get it. Why would you bring me to a hotel if you didn't want something from me?"

His eyes narrow, and his tongue darts out to wet his lips, and for some reason, my eyes fixate on it.

"I want …" His voice is dark, heavy, as though each word strains him.

He groans and throws my wrist aside, then walks to the window and slides the curtains aside to take a peek. Without moving an inch, I check out the room, the bed, the chair, the cabinet, and the hairdryer on top. The door that uses a card to lock.

A card I do not have.

I count the windows and try to peek outside to see where we are, but the curtains immediately close once his eyes land on mine.

"We will stay here," he says.

"How long?" I ask, but instead of answering, he charges to the door and turns off the lights.

The room is covered in shadow, and my heart skips a beat. I can't see anything, but I can hear him.

Suddenly, I feel his weight bear down on the bed, and I flinch.

In the darkness, all I can do is listen to the sounds.

The creaks in the bed.

The thrumming of my heart.

The rhythmic breaths … coming closer and closer.

Until his hand slips around my arm.

He pulls me with him down onto the bed, my head flopping down on a pillow, and I struggle to breathe as he drags me close to him. His hand moves down my body to my belly, and I suck in hard as he pushes me against him … against his half-hard bulge.

A rumbling groan emanates from his throat, and my skin erupts into goose bumps.

His mouth is right at the nape of my neck, every breath of his making me whimper.

"Don't. Move."

His voice is low and commanding, and I dare not disobey.

So I stay put, eyes wide open, as he slowly descends into a deep and long slumber, his hand still possessively splayed over my belly as if this killer without a name means to say … *mine*.

Four

Aurora

I don't sleep.

Not for an entire night.

Who would ever be able to with a giant snoring right next to them?

All I can do is breathe in and out against the palm of his hand, which is splayed against my belly. Every breath is delayed because each time I do, I feel him against me, pressing into me, making me hyperaware of the fact only mere inches of fabric are between our naked bodies.

I swallow down the lump in my throat.

He snores again.

I shouldn't stay here. I should try to find an exit and make a run for it.

I peer over the edge of the bed but see nothing in the darkness of the night. There's no way I'll find a way out without moving.

Maybe he won't notice if I slip out from underneath his arm.

Sweat drops roll down my back as I inch forward and gently move my body away from his.

His body strains against mine. Another groan follows.

And then his arm pulls me closer again.

All that effort for nothing.

I breathe out a sigh, but I swallow it again the second I feel his breath deep in the nook of my neck.

And my cheeks start to glow.

Oh God.

Don't even think about it.

I close my eyes and force the image of his lips against my skin to disappear.

Why does it have to be like this?

One moment, I'm playing the piano, and then the next, I'm lying in bed with the man who killed all our family guards and almost murdered my father.

Almost,

But where could my father be?

Did he run off to a secret hideout? Will he come to save me?

And if he does, could he win against this lumbering

giant?

I shiver at the thought of my father fighting this beast of a man.

I don't want him to get hurt.

But I don't want to end up in this beast's clutches either.

Papa always said he'd keep me safe, so why isn't he here?

He wouldn't have abandoned me, right?

My body turns stone cold at the thought.

No, he's out there, thinking of ways to get me back. I'm sure of it.

But I don't know if it's the prospect of my father fighting this man or the fact that every breath of his against my neck sends a chill down my spine.

I know he can feel me moving away. One inch and his hand firms up against my body. So I do the only thing I can do. I roll over to face the ceiling. At least then I won't have to face my own body's reaction to being shoved up against his package.

Suddenly, a buzzer goes off, and my eyes find his in the darkness.

We stare at each other for a moment.

My heart pounds in my throat as he stares back at me, fully awake.

His hand still resting on my belly, where it feels like butterflies fly all around.

Then he slides his hand off me and picks up a phone to stop the buzz. Within two seconds, he's up and about, throwing open the curtains as I sit up straight and blink a couple of times to adjust to the sudden burst of light entering the room.

He clutches the window and stares outside for a good while. Almost like a statue basking in the early morning rising sun.

I slip off the bed in silence and sneak into the bathroom, but the second I touch the door, his voice booms through the room. "Don't."

Of course, he has eyeballs in the back of his head.

Sighing, I leave the door open and go to the sink to take a much-needed sip. But when I look up into the mirror, the girl I see makes me do a double take. She's covered in black smudges from all the tears, eyes red and puffy, lipstick all smudged. Good God.

I quickly rinse my face with a tissue and some water and wipe away the excess makeup, then dry myself off. I can't wash my hands with these gloves on, but that can wait. First, I need to get rid of him.

When I rise again my eyes come into contact with his through the mirror, and it makes me jolt.

He's just standing there, casually leaning against the doorjamb with his arms crossed, staring me down.

I turn to face him, the collar around his neck drawing my attention, but I dare not ask about it. "So what now?"

His brows rise like he's waiting for me to answer my own question.

I swallow. "I need to pee."

"Do your business."

I frown. He can't be serious, right?

Is he actually expecting me to pee in front of him?

"Can you at least turn around?"

"So you can stab me?" he quips, and a hint of a smile briefly makes his lips twitch. "No."

So he wants to watch?

Damn this guy.

I suck in a breath and waltz to the toilet, staring him down for another second before I pull down my underwear and sit on the seat in the blink of an eye. But not fast enough, it seems, because he clearly looked, judging from the glint in his eyes and the tongue dipping out to lick the seam of his lips again. And I am struggling to keep the blush at bay.

He keeps looking at me, and for a second, I contemplate holding my pee. But I have to go so badly. I've held it all night and can't do it anymore.

So I let it out even though he never stops watching me.

The relief is instant, but it's instantly replaced by shame.

No one has ever watched me like this while I do my private business.

Let alone the fact that he's looking at me like he wants to either kill me or eat me up like a snack.

I swallow away the nerves and clean up as best I can without revealing too much of myself, but it's hard to do so with my legs closed tightly. The thought of him watching makes it hard for me to focus. I never once imagined someone could watch me like that, let alone the fact that it's an actual killer.

Not that anyone has ever looked at me.

Especially not a man as buff as him.

I clear my throat and get up, slipping my underwear back on so I can quickly pat down my black dress and pretend nothing happened.

Then I approach him while trying not to make a hasty move that'll set him off. He stays put against the doorpost, his eyes on me like a hawk as I come to stand in front of him.

"Can I at least go back into the room?"

"We're leaving," he says.

I frown. "Oh …"

Wherever he's taking me, it can't be good.

I have to try to get out of this.

"Like I said, my father is wealthy. Maybe he can arrange something, and—"

"Hands," he interrupts.

I don't dare to defy him. Not when I know he's got that knife in his pocket, ready to use at any moment. He'd be able to kill me in a blink of an eye. He's done it before with my father's guards. One after the other, they all fell like mere flies in his way.

This man is not someone you mess with if you're not willing to risk your life.

And I definitely want to stay alive.

So I raise my hands.

He pulls another tie wrap from his pocket and flicks it

over my wrists, sealing them together, and my pulse quickens.

"Please, I won't be difficult. You don't have to do this," I say.

He swallows, jaw tensing up again. "Turn around."

It takes me a few seconds to do as he asks, as I feel queasy already.

Suddenly, he throws a new bag over my head and tightens it at the base, forcing me to breathe in and out through tiny holes again.

Oh God.

"No, no, please!" I beg. "Not this bag again! Please, take it off."

But my cries fall on deaf ears as he lifts me from the floor and throws me over his shoulder again, marching out of the room we spent the night in.

Probably never to return again.

Five

BEAST

The ride back to the house is strenuous. Too long.

My mind never stops going in circles, thinking about the killings, the escaped target of my job… and her.

The girl who made me stop.

The girl in the back of my van, pleading for me to let her go.

I cannot.

Even though her soft whimpers go through marrow and bone.

It shouldn't bother me. I'm a killer. A beast. A hound with a single purpose: hunt and retrieve.

But she … she vexes me to the point when I'm no longer myself.

My fingers tighten around the steering wheel as I pull up into the parking lot of my owner's mansion. I won't have to deal with her for much longer, but the thought of having to hand her over is making me want to roar.

I wish I'd never seen her.

But it's too late for wishes now.

She cries again, and even though I can't physically see her, I still see her in my mind. Her face stained with tears, lips smeared, eyes puffy, with a face begging me not to do the very thing I'm about to do.

The one thing I'm forced to do.

Return.

With or without her.

But I made a choice, and now I have to stick with it.

Grumbling, I kick open my door and jump out, then slide open the van. She huddles in the corner, knees pulled up to her chest, her panties peeking through underneath her black dress, and I can't help but zoom in on them.

My cock twitches in my pants.

Don't. He'll know.

I push the feeling aside and grab her by the feet, pulling her out. She shrieks, in vain, because we both know whatever she says or does won't work on me.

I throw her over my shoulder with ease, and she kicks and punches me yet again as if she's given up the meek-lamb shtick and now wants to prove she's not going to come quietly.

"Let me go!" she yells as I march toward the side entrance and a maid opens the door.

I ignore her scratching my back, which feels like tiny cat claws, and bring her into the hallway.

"Where are we?" she yells. "And why does my voice echo?"

I don't answer. Instead, I wait for the maid to come back.

"He's back?" My owner's voice booms through the room next to the stairs. "Make him come in."

The maid comes back and nods at me, so I proceed.

My steps are heavy with shame and worry about what's to come, but I know I must face my mistakes. One of them is thrown across my shoulder as we speak.

"Put me down!" the girl yells.

And I do. Not because she asks, but because I'm right in front of my owner, and he doesn't look pleased.

"What is this?" he asks.

"A prisoner," I say, my fingers digging into her shoulders so she won't try to run off or harm anyone.

His eyes are stern as he looks up at me from his desk. "I thought I told you to kill them all."

"Yes, sir."

"Then why haven't you?" he asks, his voice riddled with bitterness.

I clear my throat. "My target escaped."

"*Escaped?*" My owner's eyes start to twitch. "You …"

That's the one.

The voice that can break even a man like me.

Because I know what happens when that voice appears.

Suddenly, his eyes settle on the girl. "Guards. Take her to the waiting room and keep watch." Then he focuses his angered gaze back on me. "I will deal with this beast first."

**

Aurora

A rough hand on my shoulder pushes me forward, shoving at my back when I don't move quickly enough. I struggle to keep up, not being able to see a thing as we walk. Suddenly, he throws me down, and I shriek.

I'm on a hardwood floor.

My heart is beating a million times an hour.

I lift my head to listen to the sounds around me.

"Stay there," a man says.

Footsteps move in the opposite direction, and then a door slams shut.

I breathe in and out a couple of times to calm myself, but it's impossible when I can't see and can't properly use my hands. I'm trapped in someone's house, and God only knows what they plan on doing with me.

I have to get out.

I crawl up from the floor on my knees by propping my

hands underneath me, ignoring the man's words. I push myself up and walk around the room, bumping into all sorts of things—tables, chairs, cabinets—until I hit a wall.

With my hands held in front of me, I feel my way across to the door and rummage the handle, but of course it's locked.

"Dammit," I mutter to myself.

I continue feeling my way along the wall, but there doesn't seem to be any other door, only a window. But maybe if I can get it to open, I can jump outside.

I bend over and fish around for a handle until I find one and try to push it open, but it's tough when your wrists are tied together, and you have no idea what you're doing.

A sudden roar from the other room makes me stop and turn to listen.

WHACK!

I jolt, my ears barely able to take the sound.

Because it definitely did not sound like a hand … but a whip.

WHACK!

Another muffled roar fills the rooms, and I struggle to breathe from the sound alone.

It's awful. And every strike is followed by a cry in pain.

And all of it is happening in the same room I just got pushed out from.

WHACK!

Each strike makes tears form in my eyes because the sheer pain in the howl that follows is too much to take.

So much so that I cover one of my ears with my tied wrists and push my other ear up against the wall just so I don't have to listen to the sounds.

After a while, it ends, and my cheeks are stained with tears, rubbing against the bag around my head. I don't know what went down there, but it was definitely violent. And even though I'm used to the violence in this world, listening to someone being punished with sickening pain is never easy.

I suck in a breath and push away from the wall, lowering my hands too.

I've wasted too much time. I need to find a way out before it's too late.

My hands immediately dive back to the window, searching for a way to open it.

Suddenly, the door behind me slams open again.

"What do you think you're doing?" a man roars.

I shriek and hurry to push it open, but just as I've made a small opening, someone wraps his muscular arms around my body and whisks me away.

"Let go of me!" I yell, punching and kicking as best as I can, but these men seem impervious to pain.

"Stay quiet," the man says, hauling me back into the same room I was in moments ago. I may not be able to see, but I have a clear memory of the path I took. And not only that, but this room carries that same god-awful smell as the one before. Like someone sprayed way too much cologne.

Suddenly, a cold, sharp thing presses against my neck.

"Don't move or speak unless told. Do you understand?"

I swallow and nod.

The blade is removed, and the hood is ripped off my head.

I struggle to take a breath with the bright light pointed at my face from the desk behind which a man watches me.

"So you're Blom's daughter?"

I nod.

"Speak up, girl," the man says.

"Yes," I say, and my lips part again to ask why he'd bring me here and what he wants with me, but then I remember the words of the man who took me back into this room, and I don't want to get cut into pieces.

So I shut up and listen.

"What's your name?"

"Aurora," I reply.

"Aurora … such a beautiful name," he muses, licking his lips profusely. "I'm surprised he didn't offer to trade you."

Bile rises in my throat.

"Wh-Who are you?" I mutter.

The man smiles. Viciously. "My name is Lex De Vos."

Lex De Vos. Why does it sound so familiar yet—

Wait. I remember. My father once mentioned his name when he was talking about a shipment and a large sum of money.

"Where is your father?" His stern voice interrupts my train of thought.

Lex must be responsible for the attack on our house.

For killing all of my father's guards and his guests.

My whole body begins to shake. "I don't know."

Lex snorts. "Of course you don't."

My eyes squint from the light. "I don't, I swear. I don't know where he is."

He smacks his flat hand on the table. "DON'T LIE TO ME!"

I jolt from the sudden outburst. "I'm sorry. I don't know. I'm telling you the truth."

"But you were there," he says through gritted teeth.

"Yes, I was home. I was playing the piano," I say, word-vomiting my way through this conversation to stay alive. "I don't know what happened, but suddenly, there was smoke and gunfire all around, and then some giant man came in to try to kill my papa, and I tried to shoot him, so he came after me, and then Papa vanished, and this guy took me to—"

"ENOUGH!"

I shut up immediately.

"I don't need your life story. I need your father. Now. And if you won't tell me where he is …"

I shake my head. "Please, I don't want to die."

The light in front of me is lowered. "You think I care what you want?" Lex growls. "My dog brought you here, so what should I do with you now? Feed you to him?"

My eyes widen, and I gasp in shock.

Lex laughs maniacally. "What a joke. I tell him to bring a head, and he brings me a pussy instead." He shakes his head.

"Useless."

"My father will come to rescue me," I blurt out in anger.

A guard behind me immediately rushes toward me with the knife he just threatened me with, and I brace for defense, but then the man in front of me holds up his hand and the guard stops.

Lex's eyebrows rise in a taunting manner. "You think so?"

I swallow away the lump in my throat as he taps his fingers onto the desk.

"I think he's a coward who ran with his tail between his legs and would rather leave behind everything he owns than come back and risk his pitiful fucking life."

Teeth clenched, I fight the tears.

"Oh, I know what your father is like, Aurora."

"You know nothing about my family," I say through gritted teeth.

He snorts again. "We'll see about that." He throws a look at the guard. "I've heard enough. Put her in the cell. Maybe she'll learn a thing or two about real life outside those fucking spray-painted gold walls of that fucker's house."

My eyes widen.

What cell? Where? How long?

"No, I didn't do anything," I sputter.

Lex smiles wickedly, and he caresses his beard. "You don't need to do anything, Aurora. Just exist, and your father will come crawling back to me to settle this debt once and for all."

Before I can say anything, the guard already has his hands around my waist. "Don't touch me!" I shriek as he throws me over his shoulder. "Let go of me!"

But my cries fall on deaf ears as he carries me out of the room and down the hallway, where there's a heavily locked door. "Got another one."

Another one?

Someone else is down there?

Another guard unlocks and opens the door, and the man carrying me stomps down the stairs into pitch-black darkness.

"Please, not in here. Anywhere but here," I beg, feeling like the darkness around me is swallowing me whole. The door at the top of the stairs with all the light is farther and farther away, and then we turn a corner.

In the room is a giant cell with thick iron bars capable of holding a human. A beast.

In it is a single toilet without a cover, a sink, a crevice that can be used as a bed, and a drain.

The worst kind of prison I've ever seen.

The guard puts me down and holds my wrists with one hand while opening the cell with a key. "Be a good fucking girl, and don't make this harder on yourself than it already is. Cooperate," the guard growls.

"I'm not going to be your willing victim," I tell him.

He shoves me into the cell hard enough to make me fall, and I can't catch myself with my hands, so I fall face-first into the hard concrete. I cry out in pain, hissing from the scratches on my cheek while the guard behind me locks the door to the cell, sealing me inside.

"Keep it up, and maybe you won't need to be willing at all," he taunts.

I don't even want to know what that entails. If it's a bluff or an actual threat.

"Maybe the boss will keep you here forever," the guard jests, lowering his head to meet my gaze. "As a pet."

My pupils dilate, and I shake my head.

"Please, no—"

"Don't beg me. Beg him," he says, pointing at a corner in the cell. "You'll be his toy now."

Toy?

His?

As the guard backs away and walks back up the stairs, my entire body begins to quake. Because all I can do is stare at the corner … and the smoldering green eyes looming in the darkness. A beast … waiting to swallow me whole.

Six

BEAST

When our eyes connect, I instantly know ...

I want to keep her.

I step forward, but that single move makes her crawl back until she hits the wall.

Still scared, even more than before.

I pause and watch her from my corner, tilting my head for a better view.

The door at the top of the stairs is closed, and what light remains filters through a tiny hole underneath the door, barely enough to illuminate even a speck of dust.

But I see her.

In the darkness, I come alive.

My eyes have grown used to the shadows that inhabit this cell. The scents. The sounds.

And I definitely smell and hear her.

Lemon zest with a hint of honey. A perfume that wafts through the air every time she so much as flinches because of one little look.

But I won't stop looking.

Her soft breaths are like music to my ears, and I close my eyes so I can enjoy it more, the sound making me groan with delight.

Oh, I can't fucking wait to hear more.

I lick my lips and approach her slowly. She's cowering in the corner, desperately trying to get away, but there is no escaping this hell of mine I call home. This cell is where she belongs now. And maybe what that guard said was true.

Maybe she is a toy for me.

A plaything sent by my owner.

A gift to make up for his violence and to make me more compliant.

A wretched smile forms on my lips at the thought of making her mine. Of touching her, using her body, making her yield until she whimpers like before.

My cock tents in my pants, but I will it down as I inch closer. All she does is stare up at me with wide eyes, like a deer caught in headlights. And I can't help but kneel in front of her and lean in to touch her face. There's a red mark from her fall when the guard pushed her, and the mere sight of this blemish on my pretty toy makes me want to rip off his limbs and eat them while he watches.

But the guard is gone now, and we are all who remain.

I'm so close, I can almost taste her, my heart beating faster and faster. I can think of nothing else but to touch her, and I don't understand why. Why there's this need growing inside me.

My hand slides down her face, and she shudders in place as I grip her chin. She turns her head, but it won't stop me from inching even closer and reveling in her scent right at the base of her neck. She smells so nice, and it makes me want to bury my nose in her hair and lick the salty droplets of sweat off her skin.

Suddenly, a hand rises out of nowhere to slap me, but I grip her wrist just in time. She glances at me through the corner of her eye, her body shaking underneath mine as I tower over her.

I don't know why she tries to fight me.

Doesn't she feel the very same thing I do?

Veins pulsing with heat, desperate to find out why?

She whimpers again as my grip on her wrist grows tighter. "Please …"

And for some reason, it makes me pause.

I never pause.

Not with any of my victims.

But she … she's not my victim.

She's a prize.

And to hear her cry out like that stops me in my tracks.

I've never cared for any cries, but hers … they touch something in my body I didn't know existed. As if it's the very last thing on this goddamn earth I'd ever want to hear.

She gazes at me in awe, her eyes growing bigger and bigger as if she's terrified of me, and I don't like that look one bit.

Fear is the last thing I wanted to instill in her.

So I release her wrist and back away as slowly as I came, ensuring my movements don't startle her. But when I'm back in my corner, she's still frozen to the ground, staring at me like I'm the one man who will destroy whatever she has left.

And I don't understand.

Because when we were in that hotel room, I saw her looking at me, my ripped body … the thick cock hiding in my pants. I know for a fact she wanted to touch it.

Just like I do every night.

And it took every ounce of my self-control not to take her up on that offer and feel her hands wrap around my dick.

Just like she offered and almost begged me to.

She wanted to please me.

So then why would she be scared of me now?

***

Aurora

I shudder in the corner, unable to move. Not because I'm terrified of what might happen to me, but also because of how close I let him come ... and how impossible it suddenly became to breathe.

The second his hand touched my skin, my body reacted in a way I've never felt before.

Like all it wanted to do was give in.

Let this man touch me.

Sniff me.

Taste me.

I suck in a ragged breath.

No way can I let a man like him get close again.

Holy shit, that was intense.

My heart is still thumping in my throat just from him being mere inches away from me, sliding his fingers down my face. And now I'm not sure anymore whether my skin burns from the scrape or his touch.

Why did my body respond the way it did?

I want to shake it off, but I fear every move I make will backfire.

I don't know how I got the courage to try to slap him.

Or where I got the idea that it would actually keep a savage like him at bay.

Because that's just it ... this man is no man. Even the

guy he works for called him a beast.

And now I'm here, sharing a cell with this very same beast.

Good God. Things could not get any more difficult than they already are.

One moment, I'm trying to live the life Papa envisioned for me, and then the next, my house is destroyed, my father almost murdered, and I'm swept away by some rugged animal, brought to a mafia lord, and locked in a cage.

Tears well up in my eyes, but I wipe them away and tug at my gloves to ensure they stay on.

I have to figure out a way to get out of here.

But that beast in the corner keeps watching me, and something tells me he's not going to let me escape that easily. He works for that mafia lord. Judging from the hawkish look in his eyes, he definitely won't let me out of his sight.

And I don't understand why … why he would do this to me?

Why he would bring me in front of his boss like that and then get me thrown in this cell?

And why is he locked up in here too?

I mean, I'm the daughter of that asshole's enemy. Of course, Lex would want to keep me as collateral. Wait until my father shows up so they can negotiate. Use me as leverage. And I obviously won't comply willingly.

But this beast … he's in here with me like he deserves punishment too, and I don't understand why.

I take a peek at his face, but it's so hard to see in the darkness. All I can see are his eyes, his lips … and the giant scar on his face running from his brow to his chin. And for a second, I wonder what he had to go through to get that.

That's when I notice an extra wound beside the other scar.

It's fresh and bloody.

And it definitely wasn't there before.

Someone did that to him. But when? And why?

My eyes lower down to his neck, realizing something is missing. The collar.

Stop caring so much. You're going to get yourself killed.

I avert my eyes and try not to move, even though I'm shaking, and I don't know if it's from the cold or the way this guy looks at me.

I shouldn't let it get to me.

This guy is a murderer.

He killed all my family's guards and tried to kill my father and me.

I'm lucky I escaped death.

I can only hope Papa is out there, looking for me, devising a plan to get me out of here.

Because the longer I stay here, the more I realize how precarious my situation is.

With every passing second, this threat looming in the darkness becomes bigger. The man in the shadows, waiting to chew me up and spit me out like the goddamn toy the guard said I was.

But then why can't I stop thinking about the fact that when he looked me in the eyes, he actually backed away?

I frown. I guess I should be glad. Although I'm more in shock than anything else. Because when that guard threw me in here, I was sure I was a goner.

This man in front of me was supposed to make me talk.

Spill the beans about whatever, my father's money, his location, anything that boss of his wants even though I have no clue regarding any of it.

Yet … he has not moved since he touched me.

I quietly sigh and push back more tears.

There's no point in pondering when I don't have answers, and I am definitely not going to ask him.

For now, I have no other choice but to remain weary at all costs and focus on my escape. That's all that matters.

Despite the fact that I'm exhausted from everything that happened and haven't slept for a single second since this beastly man laid eyes on me.

I have to keep my eyes open. No rest.

Because if I fail, if I fall asleep even for a moment …

The beast will awaken.

Seven

BEAST

I lie down on my makeshift bed made of straw and a few pieces of old clothing. It's not at all as comfortable as the hotel bed we spent the night in, but I know how to make it work.

This is what I'm used to. And that one night at the hotel is better left where it belongs; in my memories.

Still, it's hard to stop thinking about that comfortable bed. About her curled up beside me, her hair so soft and prickly against my face as I take in her scent.

My cock grows hard at the mere fantasy of touching her, of sliding my hand down her waist and thighs, of slipping between her legs and feeling her get wet.

God, it's been too long. So fucking long my cock tents in my pants, ready to take what's been occupying my every waking thought.

Her.

The girl from the picture, the girl I snatched out of her home filled with riches, so I could bring her to my owner, just because I failed at doing the only job I was born to do.

Groaning, I turn to look at her.

She's still in that same corner, her legs pulled up tightly against her chest like she did in the van. I haven't seen her move, let alone speak.

Maybe she's afraid.

Afraid of what I might say.

What I might do if she says something I don't like.

She's right to be suspicious. I can be anyone's worst fucking nightmare if I let myself go. But for now, I'm calm. Content.

Because she is here … with me.

And however selfish that may be, it's the best thing that's happened to me in a long fucking time.

I close my eyes and picture her in front of me, her doe-like eyes staring up at me from the bed as she unclasps my belt, my dick straining at the fabric from the mere promise of being touched by a pretty little creature like her.

In my mind, no one can watch.

No one but me knows what happens.

And *nothing* is forbidden.

A filthy smile forms on my face as I imagine her pulling out my ample length and rubbing me long and gently, until her cheeks get flustered and her lips perk up, and I lean in to claim them.

My eyes burst open.

There she is.

In the flesh.

But not at all as willing as in my fantasies.

Unfortunate.

Even though I knew somewhere, deep down, she'd be apprehensive.

Grumbling to myself, I close my eyes again and focus on the one thing that keeps me going.

Sleep.

Because when I wake, a new day has started.

And dawn always means another job, another shot at what I truly want.

A second chance at life.

***

Going to sleep and waking pass in the blink of an eye.

At least, it feels that way for me.

Because when my eyes open, they immediately catch the eyes of the girl still cowering in the corner, twitching, widening, as though she's deathly scared again now that I've awakened.

Has she not moved all night?

Frowning, I stay still and just look at her for a while, wondering how a girl like her could ever deal with such little sleep. Not even I can handle more than forty-eight hours, and that's stretching it.

But she's been awake for more than that now.

I know because when I lay beside her in that hotel bed, I could feel her body tense every time I so much as moved a muscle.

She's been forcing herself to stay awake ever since I came into her life and swept her away.

All because of her fear for me…

But I'm not the one she needs to fear the most.

I clear my throat and sit up straight, and her body instantly freezes. I don't want to scare her, but I guess my physical appearance makes that a tough job.

My stomach growls, and I look down, then back up to the cell's railing. There isn't much activity upstairs, which is strange. Typically, someone always comes to check in on me right about now.

I wait while the girl's big eyes are on me at all times.

I wonder if she stared at me like that all night.

If she's thought about me at all since I stole her away.

I swallow and look at the door once more, growing more impatient with every passing second. More growling ensues, and my lips begin to twitch.

It's morning, and I'm hungry. It's breakfast time, and the guards know this. The routine is the same every day. So then why aren't they here yet?

I get up, and the girl flinches, backing away into the darkest corner as I begin pacing around the cell. I'm trying to keep my cool, but it's getting harder by the second. Every time I pass her, she looks up at me with big, innocent eyes, and I hate it because it makes me want to lash out in anger.

Where is my goddamn food?

The girl keeps looking at me every time I turn to march toward her along the railing, and I stop midway there to stare her down.

"WHAT?" I bark.

She jolts, then shakes her head as tears well up in her eyes.

And for some reason, it stings in a place where I've not felt pain in a long while.

What does it mean?

"Answer me," I growl.

Even in complete darkness with only a sliver of light coming into the room from underneath the door, I can still see the slight blush on her cheeks.

"N-Nothing," she mutters.

She avoids my gaze. Like a wounded prey desperate to draw attention away from itself. And I realize then and there I may have only made her fear me more.

I sigh out loud and close my eyes for a second attempting my very best to ignore the strain in my stomach after such a brutal day of work.

I walk toward her, and her eyes immediately widen as her body begins to shiver. I crouch down in front of her and tilt my head. She's so pretty up close. Like a broken doll that needs mending.

And even though I have nothing in this cell to help her with, I still want to reach out and make her feel better. So I lean in, even though she huddles farther and farther away, shuddering, breathing ragged breaths. I grab her hair and bring it to my nose, taking a deep whiff. The scent is like an aphrodisiac and almost makes my eyes roll into the back of my head.

I groan with delight as my eyes open again, and all I see is beauty right in front of me.

Yet she seems so far away still, shivering in place.

I groan, my cock hard as a rock as I scoot closer and invade her space. When I look at her from up close, all I can think about is touching her and pressing my lips onto hers.

I don't understand what it means.

I've never had these feelings before.

And she definitely doesn't want me the same way.

But maybe ... I can *make* her feel the same way.

***

AURORA

He's so close that I can almost feel his breath on my skin.

I shudder, unable to breathe, let alone think.

I'm transfixed by the way he looks at me, his gaze so overpowering I don't know how to move away even though I definitely should.

His finger grazes my cheek as he grabs a strand of my hair and takes another whiff, just like before. And every time he does, a rumbling groan emanates from deep within his chest, as though the mere scent of my hair arouses him.

I swallow away the lump in my throat.

Sweat drops roll down my forehead as he gets even closer until I'm almost convinced he's going to lick my neck.

I feel like he wants to devour me.

But why?

This man showed no interest in me back in the hotel room, despite my attempts at seducing him. He stopped me right as I was about to offer myself to him in exchange for my safety. My freedom.

Instead, he brought me here and got me locked up, and now he's suddenly interested?

It doesn't make any sense.

Yet I can't shake this feeling like all he's wanted to do since he laid eyes on me was make me irrevocably his.

His hand slides down my face, my neck, every caress causing a wave of electricity along my spine. I shudder when his hand travels down my shoulder and my arm until he reaches my glove ... and curls his finger underneath to pull it.

I quickly jerk my hand from his grip and swat him away. "Don't."

His nostrils flare, and he glares at me, incensed.

I push myself up against the wall, clearing my throat. "Just … stay away."

His lips part, the scar drawing my attention more than anything. Until he speaks. "You're scared."

I frown, but it quickly turns into a scowl. "Of course I am."

He stretches out a hand. "Why?"

I stare at him, stupefied why he'd even ask. "You tried to kill my father." I pause to let the gravity of my words sink in. "You killed his guards. My friends."

My voice comes out like a whine, but it's the pain and fear all coming out at once.

"Friends?" he parrots, inching back to give me some space.

"Yes," I say, swallowing away the tears.

"What are friends?"

I frown, terribly confused. How … how does he not know what friends are?

He must be joking, right? This must be a lie. It has to be.

I snort, and it ends up in full-blown laughter. "You're kidding me, right?"

But he merely stares at me with disdain as though I'm mocking him, and it instantly makes me stop laughing. "You really don't know?"

He shakes his head, frowning, his nostril twitching like he's offended I'd even question his reality. But who in the world doesn't know what friends are?

"How? How do you not know?" I ask.

He shrugs, averting his eyes as he kneels farther away from me.

"You don't have *any* friends?"

"I don't know what you mean," he says.

"People," I explain.

"People … like my owner," he mutters.

His owner? Does he mean the man who sent him to assassinate my father and take me with him?

"No, I mean people you like. You know, people you talk to."

He shakes his head. "The guards … talk to me sometimes."

I gasp. "Those guys aren't your friends. They're keeping you as a prisoner in this cell, just like me." I look around at the bars surrounding us. "Friends wouldn't do this. Friends are nice. They make you happy."

"Then I don't have them," he says.

No friends.

My God.

I mean, I didn't have many, and most of them were people working for my papa, but to have no friends at all … no one to talk to … "Wow."

"What?" He raises a brow.

"Nothing," I mutter, trying not to anger him any more than he already has.

He's been pacing around so much in this cell. I know

something is bothering him, but I don't understand what. It's almost like he's been waiting for someone, and I assumed it must be someone he likes to talk to. But maybe that's out of the question too.

The beastly man gets up, suddenly towering over me again, and I shudder in disbelief at how huge he really is. Then he turns and marches back to where he's been sleeping. There he continues to stare at me, almost as if he's wondering why I won't let him get close. But I don't think I'd be able to resist if I did. If he'd even allow me to.

This kind of man takes what he wants without regard for anyone else's feelings or wishes.

Even a girl like me.

Goose bumps scatter on my skin.

So then why did he move away from me?

He sighs. "Friends are a weakness."

I blink a couple of times to interrupt my own thoughts. "Why would you say that?"

He gazes up at me from underneath his eyelashes, the thick gash on his face making me swallow. "Your friends died, so now you are angry."

Oh wow.

"Of course I am," I say, emotions making my voice high pitched.

"Emotions. Friends. They're a weakness."

Well, that's cold.

"They didn't deserve to die."

"No one does," he replies. "But everyone dies. In the

end."

I blink a couple of times. Even with such little words, he still manages to make me think about them.

He fishes his knife from his pocket. The same one he stabbed my papa with, and the mere sight makes me freeze. "The only question is … how." He twirls it around between his fingers like a plaything. "Life and death. It's all the same to me."

"You're wrong."

I don't know where I get the courage to speak up, but I do.

"Life in here? It is death," he explains.

"Life could be so much more than this," I say. "You make it sound like it's black and white. It's not."

"Then tell me what life is to you," he says.

My fingers scratch along the concrete floor. I don't know if I should, but I can't help myself. "Life can be beautiful. Rough. Idyllic. Painful. Sweet. It is a spectrum of emotions and experiences, and if you never once tried to feel any of it, then how can you know it's all the same?" I say.

He's silent for a while.

Like he's taking in my words and letting them simmer in his brain.

"I don't know," he says after a while, and he looks away, lowering the knife as if he's been defeated.

I frown in disbelief, shaking my head, and I sigh out loud. "You were so sure of yourself a few seconds ago, and now?"

"I'm not sure of anything anymore," he says, looking me directly in the eyes. "Not since I met you."

A blush spreads across my face, despite my contempt for this man who destroyed my life. I don't want my skin to flush, but I can't stop it either. And I can't help but wonder if these emotions he perceives as weakness are the only reason I'm alive.

"Emotions are not weakness," I say. He licks his lips, and I don't know why I focus on it the way I do. "I'm alive because of emotions. Emotions *you* felt."

His lip twitches, and his jaw tightens. "Trouble. That's what they cause." He tosses his knife up and down a few times. "I don't need more. I have enough."

"Well, you made the choice, not me," I spit, mildly offended he regrets his decision not to kill me.

"I'm glad I did," he says, and it instantly draws my attention back to his penetrative eyes. "Even though I suffered for it."

Suffered?

I gasp.

Does he mean the extra wounds?

"I ..." I don't even know what to say, so I close my mouth again and opt for nothing at all.

Because I couldn't possibly think of thanking this brute for saving me after trying to kill me and getting me in this miserable cell.

"I don't need pity. I don't need anything," he growls.

"No friends. Nothing. Just this knife and my gun." He closes his eyes and sucks in a breath. Right then, something roars, but it's not a voice. It's definitely a stomach.

His.

"And food," he groans.

Is that why he's so upset and pacing?

Because he's hungry?

"You're hungry," I mutter.

His eyes narrow, but he refuses to answer.

"Why don't you demand some food?"

He tilts his head at me like I'm saying something absolutely ridiculous.

"You're a giant," I add. "You must have some leverage, right?"

His lip tips up into an inkling of a smirk, and for some reason, it makes my heart beat faster. "This cell is my home. What makes you think I have power?"

I swallow.

Maybe he's right. We're both in here for a reason.

Though I can't fathom what this man must've done to end up in this situation.

Let alone the fact that somehow, someway, someone managed to tame a beast of his size. Just to be able to use him as a personal attack hound. And judging from the way he's adjusted to the darkness, the way he's been looking at me all calm and collected, sleeping on mere straws, and not having a care in the world about any of this … he's grown quite used to it.

And that begs the question … A question I haven't dared to ask. But I must know.

"How long have you been in here?"

It takes him a while to answer, but when he does, my stomach wants to flip over. "Years."

Eight

Aurora

I sit and stare, tipping back and forth on my butt while clutching my legs. I try not to go insane. I truly do. But I've never wanted to sleep as badly as I do now.

My eyes open and close slower and slower, and I yawn.

Good God, I've never felt this tired before.

Every time I blink, I find it harder to open them back up again, and sometimes they don't. For a few seconds, it's bliss, as I imagine myself dozing off in my soft bed, dreaming the night away.

Then my eyes burst open, and I see the glimmer of the beastly eyes right in front of me, always lurking in the shadows, waiting to strike.

And I realize … I can't ever, ever fall asleep.

Not in here.

Not with him.

So I stay put and bounce back and forth, trying to keep myself awake while growing ever more insane.

I thought about asking him more about his life just to stay awake, but after he said that word "years," my lips felt sewn shut.

Suddenly, a loud creak at the top of the stairs captures my attention.

And his.

The man in front of me is lightning fast as he bolts to the bars to my left and clutches them with both hands, staring at the stairs. It's like he's completely forgotten I exist. At least, for now.

THWACK!

A door is slammed open, and light bursts down into this damp cell. I blink a couple of times to adjust to the light.

Someone waltzes down the stairs. The mere sound makes me shiver. I wonder what they've come to do. If they're coming for him … or for me.

It's been a full day since I last saw someone besides this beast, but I am not too happy about seeing the same guard who put me here. The wretched smile on his face makes me want to lash out.

"Hello there," he muses when he sees me. "How are you today, pretty girl?" He keeps smiling at me in a weirdly creepy way. "You know, I don't think we've had a proper introduction yet. My name is Raymond."

I don't respond. I'm far too occupied with whatever is in his hand because it's gotten that Beast to go completely haywire, tearing at the bars, ramming them with his fists. He even bites into one of them.

Good God.

Raymond's brow rises as he looks at the man in the cell with me. "What's wrong, Beast?" He pulls something from behind his back, and my eyes widen at the sight of a plate filled with red meat.

Raw meat.

And he sways it around in front of the bars like some kind of treat. Just out of reach. "Are you hungry?"

My stomach about hurtles itself out of my throat at the idea.

The man in my cell begins to growl. "Give it to me!"

"Uh-uh." Raymond swishes his finger back and forth and pulls the plate back. "Be nice."

Beast paces around, frothing at the mouth, ravenous, enraged. "Please," he says through gritted teeth after a while.

A filthy smile forms on the guard's face. "That's more like it."

And he pushes the plate underneath the bars where a tiny slit allows food to pass through. Within seconds, Beast has snatched the plate out of his hands and chomps down on the raw meat like it's nothing.

I can't stop watching him even though I should

definitely look away.

But my God, I've never seen anything like it before.

"Savage, isn't it?" Raymond says.

I don't respond. He's trying to bait me. But damn, is it hard to remain quiet.

"Whatever," Raymond mutters, and he turns around.

"Wait," I say, quickly getting up. "Isn't there more?"

"More?" He glances at me over his shoulder and laughs. "More meat?" He brings his hands to his belt buckle. "I've got plenty if that's what you want."

I wince and turn away. "Gross."

His nostrils flare, and he turns to spit on the bars, missing me by a hair. "Fuck you. You're lucky the boss kept you alive. Have fun fighting for scraps with that *thing*."

The guard walks back upstairs, and I contemplate saying something, anything, to keep him from shutting the door. Just to keep the light here.

But I can't bring myself to ask. To beg.

Still, I can't stop myself from breaking the silence and yelling, "He is not a *thing*!"

THWACK!

The door is slammed shut again, and the world has returned to darkness.

I shudder in place, tears forming in my eyes.

The only light in this room comes in through the small crevice under the door. Just enough to see the glimmer in my own damn tears as they fall down onto the ground.

Just enough … to see his reflection.

I shriek as I look up straight into his eyes.

He's right in front of me, staring me down. I stand frozen to the floor, lips quivering.

The plate is held right underneath my nose. "Do you want a bite?"

I don't even know how to respond.

One second, he's eating that stuff like a mad dog, and then he suddenly wants to share?

I shake my head.

Then my stomach growls.

There's a pause as the embarrassment makes my cheeks glow.

"You sure?" He offers it again.

My hand rises to waft it away. "No, thanks."

My stomach growls again even though it usually never does. Just my luck.

The man inches closer. Deathly close until I'm forced to lean up against the wall as he inspects me.

His finger suddenly pokes me in the belly.

I hold my breath.

"Hungry."

I shake my head again. "I'm fine."

His eyes narrow as he pushes the plate underneath my nose.

I push it back. "You take it."

He cocks his head, then turns around and walks back to his corner to sit down and munch in silence. But he never takes his eyes off me, and it makes me swallow. Hard.

He takes small nibbles of the meat now, all while watching me, almost as if he wants to show me he can be gentle too. Which makes no sense because he was destroying that meat mere seconds ago. Devouring it like he hadn't been fed in ages.

Why would he care about the way it looks now?

I slowly lower myself to the floor, squinting to see more. Even though I know I shouldn't be this intrigued, I am. There's no point in denying what's obvious.

But the fact that I can't stop watching him as much as he refuses to stop watching me should make alarm bells ring in the back of my head.

Should.

But all I can think of is how just now he wanted to share some of his food with me, despite being so obviously famished.

My stomach growls so loudly he stops eating.

And I thought my cheeks could not get any redder than they already were.

I'm so glad neither he nor I can see it in this darkness.

"You *are* hungry," he says.

"It's fine," I say. "I can handle it."

He holds up the piece of meat like it's some kind of prize. "Eat."

I raise my hand again. "No, no, I'm fine. I promise. I'll … eat another day."

That's a lie. I don't know when I'm going to eat. If ever.

But I don't want him to feel guilty for eating either.

He shrugs and takes another bite. "Another day, more meat."

I frown. "What do you mean?"

"There is no other food," he explains. "Only meat."

My eyes widen. "What?"

He swallows down some meat and puts the bones down on the plate. "I eat meat. That's it."

My jaw drops. "Wait, so you just don't eat the rest, or they never offer you anything else?"

He shakes his head. "Meat. That's it."

Meat? Just meat? How can a person live on meat alone?

"But that's not possible. You wouldn't be sitting here if that was true," I say.

He shrugs like it's no big deal.

"You'd get scurvy."

"Scurvy?" he parrots, narrowing his eyes.

"It's when you don't eat vegetables and fruits," I explain. "Your body gets sick. It needs nutrients."

"Oh …" I can see him mull it over, his eyes flicking back and forth slowly as he does. "The guard brings me pills sometimes."

I frown. So they can't even be bothered to give him the most basic human needs.

Pills. That's how his body sustains itself. And meat to fill up the rest.

Disgusting.

"Wow," I mutter.

No wonder he was so antsy and pacing around his cell

like that ... if all he ever gets to eat are scraps of meat.

Damn.

"So this is why you were angry," I say. "You didn't get food yesterday, did you?"

Beast throws me a look and then continues eating until nothing is left.

Food almost feels like a prize. A reward.

Something you need to earn.

And maybe by bringing me back instead of killing me, he did something his owner didn't like.

Beast grabs the bone and chews on it. "I like meat. It feeds my muscles."

"I can tell," I say, rolling my eyes.

A playful smile forms on his face. "My muscles?"

His chest tenses, and I don't know if he does it by accident or on purpose, but my eyes definitely go there.

I have to force myself to look away. "No, that's not what I meant, oh my God. I meant the food."

"I know." The smile is still firmly planted on his face. "You'll like it too," he says, his voice gravelly. "The meat, I mean."

Which meat?

My eyes widen, and I look away before it gets too embarrassing.

He means the red meat. The raw meat he just ate.
Not that giant thing between his legs.

This is totally not what I should be thinking about. Ever.

His lips part again. "Eventually."

The hairs on the back of my neck stand up.

Eventually.

I don't like the sound of that word.

The definitiveness.

As if he means to say ... give up hope.

"No," I say, firmly crossing my arms. "That's not food. I'll never like it, and neither should you."

"Why?"

"Your owner is mistreating you," I explain. "He should be feeding you properly cooked meals."

Beast snorts. "Me or you?" He cocks his head. "You're the hungry one, not me."

That's not fair. "Hey, I didn't ask for any of this."

"No, but you're here, might as well survive."

Survive?

Would they truly let me starve if I chose not to eat this?

No, I don't believe it. They put me here for a reason.

If that mobster wanted me dead, he would've killed me already.

"This is more than enough to survive," he adds.

"No, it's not. You're a human, and he treats you like a dog that should be happy with scraps."

I know I'm getting incensed, but I just can't fathom how a human being could do this to another. It's inhumane. It's ... beastly.

His brow rises. "Why do you suddenly care?"

I pause, feeling caught in the act. "I ... just feel like it's wrong. That's all."

He stares me down for a moment as if he's trying to see whether I'm speaking the truth. "Dog. Hound. Monster. Beast. It's all the same to me," he says, and he licks off the bone like he's savoring the very taste. "I don't care what I'm called. What I am is always the same."

He doesn't even care.

It's like he's gotten used to it.

Like he's given up the fight.

I swallow away the lump in my throat. "And what's that?"

He lowers his eyes at me and chucks the bone to the side. "A stone-cold killer."

Nine

BEAST

Killer.

That's what I am.

Whether it's humans, animals, or already slaughtered meat, I will destroy it and leave nothing in my wake.

I know my place in this world.

But her eyes ... they judge in a way that makes me feel guilty.

And that makes me stop and stare right back at them.

I've done that a lot since I found her.

Staring is all I can do when faced with regrets ... And

with unfathomable beauty.

I clear my throat, but it's impossible to look away. And it appears just as hard for her, but I don't know whether it's because of the way I look or because of the way I act.

Because the sheer look of disgust in her eyes when I ate my meal was not something I enjoyed.

She may not have wanted the meat, but I refuse to let food go to waste. And if my eating makes me a monster in her eyes, then so be it.

I've done far worse than tear apart some meat with my teeth.

Grabbing my metal cup, I carry it to the small tap near the edge of the cell and hold it underneath the water.

"A killer …" she suddenly mutters. "But you didn't kill me. Even though I tried to kill you."

I don't like to be reminded of that fact.

Not because it would've meant my end if she'd succeeded, but because I almost squeezed the life out of her.

"You hesitated," she says. "Why?"

I put down my cup and stalk toward her. But this time, she doesn't back away into the corner like she used to. She stands tall, almost as though she's daring me to answer.

Towering over her, I lean in and reach for her face. Her skin is so soft and velvety underneath my rugged finger as I slide it down her cheek until I reach the tip of her chin.

Even in the dark, her beauty never fades.

"You distracted me," I say, licking my lips as I imagine myself claiming hers.

I'm so close to her, I can almost taste her.

Her entire body erupts into goose bumps. "Distracted you?"

I don't know if I'm dreaming or if I'm fantasizing, but it's almost as if her body hovers closer to mine too.

"You remind me of something …" I murmur, gazing into her pretty eyes, wondering if there ever could've been a different choice. "Something I've always wanted."

I tip up her chin, and she shudders as my finger travels down her neck, unable to stop myself. The second I reach the crevice where her tits meet, she sucks in a breath and holds it. And it makes me wonder if she's ever been touched before.

The mere thought of being the first makes a devilish grin spread across my lips. God, I can't fucking wait to lay claim to her and be the first to fill her up.

I lean in and bring my lips to her ear, humming before I take a nibble. The sound of her whimpers is like music to my ears.

"P-Please," she mutters, her voice laced in fear.

But I know there is more to this than terror.

I can feel it from the way she looks at me. How she's been looking at me from the day we first saw each other.

She wants to yield to me.

So I grab a fistful of her hair and tilt her head back. I bury my nose in the nape of her neck and take a whiff.

"Your scent … intoxicates me," I say.

She breathes heavy breaths. "St-Stop."

My lips hover dangerously close to her skin. If it wasn't for that squeaky little voice of hers, I would've devoured her as quickly as I did the meat long ago. I can't fucking wait to kiss her, lick her skin, and suck on her peaked nipples.

God, I crave it all.

I've craved her since she tried to seduce me at the hotel, but we weren't alone.

We are now.

And I am done fucking waiting until she no longer fears me.

I grip her chin and turn her head, my tongue dipping out to lick what's mine.

She whimpers beneath me. "I'm n-not a toy."

Still some fight left in these tiny little bones.

I grin against her skin. "No, not a toy ... a prize."

Finally, I understand why she was put in this cell with me. Why my owner gave her to me.

Not as a reward for my hard work, but as an incentive to work even harder.

So I snake my arm around her waist and pull her in for a kiss.

She tastes divine, exactly the way I've imagined.

Exactly the way I hoped she would taste.

Mine.

***

Aurora

Oh my … God.

His lips are on mine.

He's actually kissing me.

I can't process what's happening because my mind is turning to mush.

It feels so good and overpowering that I don't know how to stop it. Or if I even want him to.

His free hand grips my wrist, and my eyes burst open.

I bite down.

He pulls back, releasing me from his grip, looking at me with disdain before touching his lip. It's bleeding.

Oh boy.

I did that.

"Feisty girl," he growls.

Feisty? I've never been called feisty before, not by any man.

Then again, this is no ordinary man.

"I like it."

What?

He likes it? Me?

My entire face turns red as a beet.

No, he can't *want* me like that. He made that abundantly clear in the hotel room.

Not that I care.

Besides, I only offered it there to save my life, to stop him from bringing me to this very place, and it failed. There's no reason to let him do this. No reason at all, but …

Suddenly, he leans in, his lips grazing my skin right below my ear. And everything I was thinking flies straight out the window.

It's wrong, so wrong, yet I can't even put up a fight as his lips drag a line down my neck. The rumbling groan that follows sets my body on fire.

I don't understand. He made himself very clear back in that hotel room. So then why do I get the sense he's been holding back since then?

Is it because he needed to bring me in first? Have his owner gift me to him like some pet?

Or was it something else?

"Are you scared of me?" he asks.

I don't know how to respond.

Because I definitely, very much, should be terrified.

"You're a murderer," I murmur, trying so hard not to be affected by the way his lips plant succulent kisses all over my skin. "Of course I'm scared."

"I won't hurt you." His voice is dark, heady like he's on the verge of severing whatever restraint he put on himself. And with every kiss he plants, it's becoming harder and harder to breathe.

He kisses my jaw in such a soft manner that it completely throws me off balance. Who knew a beast like him could be so gentle?

One moment, he's destroying the cage along with the meat thrown to him like he's some kind of animal, and the next, he wants to shower me in kisses. It's too confusing, too … maddening.

I must stop this before it's too late.

I instinctively plant a hand on his buff chest and push. My strength pales in comparison and does nothing except alert him. He leans back, his gaze penetrative as he places his hand on top of mine, guiding my hand down, down, down …

Until it reaches the point of no return.

I suck in another breath at the feel of his thick bulge underneath the palm of my hand. The groan that follows from deep within his throat makes me whimper out loud.

He's huge.

And hard.

Definitely as hard as a rock.

Because of me?

I gasp, partly from the shock and partly because it's exciting me in a way that should be forbidden.

I quickly remove my hand, jarred by my reaction to his body.

He's so close, I can practically taste the meat he just devoured, the scent animalistic and almost an aphrodisiac to my nostrils. Not at all what I expected. Just like this man.

And something tells me he won't go easy on me … or slow.

I gulp.

I should definitely not be thinking about that.

Definitely.

But the thought did cross my mind on several occasions.

I failed when I tried to seduce him. But what if I could try again? Would it be worth it to try to save my own life?

We're both stuck in this cell, and he shows no inclination of wanting to escape.

He may be just as evil as the men who put me here.

But do I even have a choice with him hovering so close to me?

And why does it feel like he already staked his claim?

Suddenly, the door at the top of the stairs opens again, and that same guard from before comes rushing down.

I quickly push myself as far away into a corner as I can, despite the fact that Beast is still right in front of me, sporting an obvious boner.

Of course Raymond's eyes immediately home in on it.

"Well, look at that. Does the lil doggy have a crush?" Raymond laughs, making obscene gestures that look like he's fucking the air.

I scowl at him. "No one asked you for your opinion. Or your dumb dance."

"Shut up, little girl," he growls, immediately stopping.

He fishes his key from his pocket and shoves it into the cell door, but before he turns it, he glares at the beastly man. "You. Behave. Or you'll get the collar again."

So I was right. It was a collar.

But why would they give him one?

And why does it sound like a threat?

The gate opens, and the guard eyes down Beast who only has eyes for me.

"Beast, come," Raymond commands.

Beast reluctantly removes his eyes off my body, grinding his teeth as though the mere interruption makes him want to throw hands.

He steps away, and it finally feels like I can breathe again. He follows Raymond out of the cell willingly, and Raymond shuts the door again, sealing me inside.

I can't help but grasp the bars and stare as they both walk upstairs while Raymond clenches his gun tightly.

But when the door closes and I'm left by myself, I realize there is something I'm far more scared of than anything that lumbering giant could ever do.

Pitch-black solitude.

TEN

BEAST

The moment I step into his office, I can feel the tension. It's thicker than oxygen.

Thicker even than the hard-on I was sporting mere minutes ago when I was on the verge of taking my prize.

My nostrils flare at the sight of my owner casually puffing away at a pipe near his fireplace, unaware of what he interrupted.

One day.

One fucking day…

"Beast," he says between puffs. "I take it you understand why I brought you up here?"

"No," I respond.

I don't like games. He plays too many.

He glances at me over his shoulder. "You know I don't play, right?"

Wrong.

"Yes," I lie.

"I don't like it when my men don't listen to me," he continues, throwing me a casual smile. "And I think you've learned that lesson more than any other here, haven't you?"

I nod.

"Did you enjoy your meal?"

"Yes, sir," I reply, tilting my head.

"Good." Another vicious smile follows, and he takes another puff of his cigar. "I hope you're grateful for your second chance."

I know what that was, and I know what this is.

A reminder of my place in this world.

And his ability to take everything I need to live away from me with a simple snap of his fingers.

"Thank you for the food," I reply. "I won't take it for granted."

"Will you do your job properly this time?" he asks.

I nod. "To the best of my abilities."

He pulls his cigar away and turns to look at me. "Now, you know that's not an answer. Do you want to skip another meal?"

"No, sir," I reply, staring off at the wall.

He sneers at me. "You want to eat at all?"

My fists tighten.

The prospect of losing food, the only thing that keeps me alive in that cold, harsh cell, is nothing short of maddening, and I struggle not to punch him in the throat right this very second for daring to try to take it away from me.

But I feel the eyes of the guard prodding my back, along with his gun.

I have no intention of losing my life without any gain.

Not yet ... not yet.

"You should be happy you're still alive," my owner says. "After failing my most basic order."

I don't respond.

"I've shown you how upset I am." He walks to me with calculated steps, stopping right in front of me. "So what do you intend to do about it?"

It sounds like a question, but it's really not.

Because I have no choice.

I never did.

I swallow. "I will fix my mistake."

He tilts his head, looking me dead in the eyes as he says, "Then find him."

※※※

Aurora

DRIP. DRIP. DRIP.

Water droplets falling down into the sink capture my attention. The sound they make reminds me of my own beating heart. Reminds me that I'm still alive here in the dark.

I swallow as the door is opened once more.

I don't know how long it's been since I was left here by myself, but every second is too damn long. Alone with my thoughts, nothing but silence and screams alternate in my mind, making me insane.

No wonder that beastly man became so savage.

Anyone would when faced with pure and utter darkness for hours on end.

Days.

Weeks. Months. Years.

God, how could anyone survive that long in this cold, damp cell?

I shake off the jitters, but it's no use. Especially not when two feet appear from the light upstairs, slowly coming down the steps.

When his face comes into view, my entire body erupts into goose bumps.

It's the same guard who took Beast upstairs.

The same one who locked me in here.

Raymond.

And the wretched smile on his face tells me he's up to no good.

I crawl into a corner, hoping and praying he won't see me.

But of course he already knows I'm here. It's not like I have anywhere else to go.

"Little girl, c'mon now, show your face," he jests, sauntering to the cage, dangling the key in his hand like a prize. "I know you're in there …"

"What do you want from me?" I reply.

He laughs. "Is that the way you're gonna behave? Maybe I should take this back upstairs then." He dangles a piece of bread in front of the cell, and my mouth begins to water. "And eat it myself."

He pulls it away again, making me want to run to him and snatch it out of his hands.

Which is exactly what he wants.

He's taunting me.

I can't let him get to me. Or anyone else in this house, for that matter.

"Do what you want. I don't care," I reply, looking away.

He clutches the bars. "C'mon now, I know you're hungry. I can hear your stomach all the way upstairs."

He holds out the piece of bread again, and the thought of him eating it instead of me makes me want to run at those bars and fight him for it.

Is this what that beastly man went through?

Every day?

For years?

I suck in a breath and stay put out of pure will, despite being hungry as hell.

"Such a determined girl," Raymond mutters, and he shoves the key into the lock. "Maybe you need a little more convincing."

He opens the door, and it squeaks loudly as he steps inside and closes it behind him, slipping the key back into his pocket.

Maybe I can try to steal it.

My eyes skid back and forth between the door and him, his pockets, his eyes, and the piece of bread dangling between two fingers. I feel like an animal ready to hunt.

"C'mon then, take it if you want it," Raymond says, licking his lips.

I inch forward across the concrete floor, my stomach growling at the sight of that delicious piece of bread.

And when I'm close enough, I lunge forward.

Not at the bread.

At the keys in his pocket.

My hand dives in quickly, searching, but the second I grasp them, he snags my wrist and flicks it to the side until it hurts.

"I knew it," he growls as I yelp in pain.

"Stop, you're hurting me," I say.

"Should've taken the bread," he replies. "Guess I'm gonna have to teach you a lesson in humility."

He spins me on my feet with ease, covering my mouth with one hand while the other is firmly lodged around my wrists, preventing me from moving away.

"Seems to me you like being pushed to your limits," he whispers into my ear. "Maybe I should just take what I want and make you beg for it."

Tears spring into my eyes as I vigorously shake my head.

"Then apologize," he says through gritted teeth.

But instead of doing what he asks, I bite him.

Hard.

He roars out in pain, tearing his hand off my mouth. "You fucking bit me! You bitch!"

I don't say a word. I know what I did. And I'd do it again in a heartbeat.

"Apologize!" he roars. "Or I'll make you regret you even tried."

A single tear rolls down my cheeks. "No."

His face contorts. "So be it."

Suddenly, he shoves me into the bars, my head hitting the metal so hard I see stars for a moment. I'm too disoriented to notice his hand diving underneath my dress until it has already snaked around my underwear and is pulling it down.

Oh God.

"No, don't do this," I yell.

This can't be happening. This can't be real.

"I told you, you should've taken the bread," he growls.

Suddenly, the door at the top of the stairs opens again,

and Raymond pauses.

"Please, help me," I say with tears running down my cheeks to whoever is coming down the stairs. "Don't let him do this to me."

But the second I spot that wicked old smile on that wrinkly old face, all hope of a savior vanishes.

"Got yourself in quite some trouble, little girl," Lex mutters as he struggles to get down the stairs. I hate how everyone calls me little. I am not little.

Lex's eyes fall onto his guard, who stopped groping me the minute someone started walking down the steps. "You, out."

Just two words are enough to make the guy stop. And I can't say I'm grateful, but I am relieved when his hand disappears from underneath my dress, and he steps away.

"I was just teaching her a lesson."

Lex doesn't even respond, and Raymond takes notice as he quickly unlocks the cell and steps out again.

Raymond holds up his hand to show Lex the wound. "She bit me. She fucking—"

Lex holds up his hand.

Just that, and Raymond shuts up.

Is this man that powerful?

I don't understand much about Papa's dealings, mostly because he didn't want to involve me anymore, but I knew he was messing with the wrong people.

I just didn't know how wrong.

Lex waves his hand, and Raymond runs back upstairs,

leaving the two of us all alone.

And even though Raymond was physically much stronger, Lex instills far greater fear in whoever dares to get in his way.

I gulp as he steps closer to the bars.

"Enjoying your stay? I hope the room is to your liking," he muses.

"I didn't do anything to deserve this. Let me out of here," I say.

"I don't think I'll do that. You see, I have issues with your father," he explains. "And those issues need to be resolved before I let you go."

I push back more tears. "Whatever my father did has nothing to do with me."

His brows rise. "You think?"

What?

My eyes widen in shock, but there's no time to think about his words.

"You're his daughter, and if he wants you back, he'll have to come to me." His face darkens. "On my terms."

"You just want him dead," I spit back. "And when you're done with him, you'll kill me too."

"Maybe I won't wait until after I've found your father," he retorts.

I step back from the bars.

He wouldn't.

Would he?

"You know, you should be happy you've survived," he

says. "Not many do."

What?

The hit?

This cage?

Or … Beast?

"I've put people in this cage before," he says with such a calm voice it makes the hair on the back of my neck stand up. "They barely make it through a single day."

I shudder in place. He's just trying to scare me. I won't fall for it.

"Some get torn to shreds. Others …" He licks his lips. "Eaten."

"You're lying," I say through gritted teeth.

"Am I?" He tilts his head. "Or have you just told yourself that Beast will be nice to you if you do what it wants?"

I feel like he just looked into my brain, and it scares the shit out of me.

"He's a human being," I say, incensed by his words. "And how dare you treat him like that. Feed him scraps. Raw meat. Call him 'it.' You're disgusting."

"He's an animal," he growls back. "A vicious dog, trained to do just one thing. Kill."

His words silence me.

Not because I'm terrified, but because I'm dumbfounded how a person could ever do this to another.

"He obeys *me*. And if I tell him to kill, he will kill. And if I tell him to eat …" He lowers his eyes to meet my gaze.

"He will eat."

A chill runs up and down my spine.

"So what's it gonna be, girl? Are you gonna behave?" He pulls his tissue out of his pocket and coughs loudly. "Or you gonna keep biting fingers off my guards?"

I feel like I'm about to vomit, but I force myself to keep it down.

I haven't eaten in days. Nothing to throw up anyway.

"That's what I thought," he mutters, wiping off his mouth before pushing the tissue back into his pocket. "So here's the deal. You're going to stay here, be a nice little girl, do what you're told, and maybe, just maybe, you'll survive."

"I will never, ever, help you find my father," I say.

"Oh, I don't need any help finding that rat when I have you."

My eyes widen while a smirk grows on his face.

Oh God, Papa can't come here. It's a trap. *I'm* the trap.

"No, you're lying," I say, shaking my head.

Lex's smile only grows deeper, more menacing. "No, girl, the only liar was your father when he said he had my money."

"You're sick," I hiss.

"That part is true," he replies. "But you must know, none of this would've happened if it wasn't for your father's inability to settle his debts." He clears his throat. "But I see now this little mistake my dog made might come in handy." He steps closer, almost close enough for me to grab ahold of him and try to choke him.

But that won't do me any good if I'm stuck in this cell, and the only key is with that guard who is loyal to his boss.

"Make no mistake, the only reason you're still alive is because I need your father," he says. "And you might provide the tiny bit of motivation he needs to come to me so we can settle this debt like men."

When he reaches inside the cage, I jump back.

"Hmm ... so skittish," he muses to himself. "Yet you so easily throw yourself at my dog."

What? Throw myself at him? What does he mean?

"You know, maybe I don't need your help at all ... if your father sees how well you're doing in here."

Vile. Just vile.

"I may just let my guard play with you too."

"You're despicable," I hiss.

He laughs. "Do you think I care?" The laughing abruptly stops. "Maybe you just need a little motivation too."

A shiver runs up and down my spine as he turns around and heads up the stairs.

"Have fun in there," he mutters before he slams the door shut and leaves me in the pitch-black darkness, wishing someone, anyone, would hear me scream.

Eleven

BEAST

"No, no, please, don't do this," says the man I'm dragging by the collar.

But his begging falls on deaf ears.

I'm used to my victims screaming, crying, kicking. Some even piss themselves out of sheer terror, some merely at the sight of my face.

I've learned not to react.

In fact, I don't feel anything at all when they start.

And I definitely don't feel a single thing when I throw this man onto a chair in the middle of his living room and tie him up with tie wraps.

"Please, take my money. I don't care. You can have it all," he whines as I secure his legs to the chair with the ropes I brought.

When I'm done, I stand, towering over him as I glare down.

"What do you want? If this is about Lex's money, tell him I already paid it," the man says.

"No money," I growl. "Peter Blom."

The man's eyes widen. "I don't know who that is."

Lies.

They always think they can lie to me.

That it comes without a price.

I grasp his hand, and while he screeches his head off, I cut off a finger and hold it in front of his face. "You gonna talk now?"

"Please, oh God." Saliva flows from his lips as he struggles with the pain. "It hurts!"

I grasp him by the hair and tilt his head up. "Focus!"

His eyes almost bulge out of his face. "I haven't seen him in days. What do you want with him?"

Hm. And here I thought this was a good lead.

I hold my knife across his neck. "Tell me his location."

"I don't know! I swear, I don't know!" the guy yelps.

"I won't hesitate," I growl. "Your life means nothing."

"Please, I swear on my fucking life, I don't know where he is," the man says.

"But you spoke with him, didn't you?" I push the knife into his neck. "Tell me the truth!"

Sweat drops roll down his cheeks. "Okay, okay, yes, we talked on the phone. But he didn't tell me where he was or what he was doing."

I shove the knife farther until blood oozes down his neck. "What did you talk about?"

"Money!" he gasps, whimpering as tears form in his eyes. "But I don't have it anymore. I already paid off my own debts with Lex. I couldn't give him anything, and even if I could, I wouldn't."

My nostrils flare. Not good. I need to know where he is. I don't give a damn about any kind of payment. That's not what I was sent here to do.

"Please, take it all. Whatever Lex wants, he can have it," the man mutters.

I know he's lying. I can tell from the way his lips twitch and his eyes search for anything in this room to grab ahold of, even when he's tied to a chair.

"You do know where he is," I mutter.

The guy shakes his head. "He didn't tell me where he was going."

"But you know where he was when he called you," I retort.

The guy starts to shiver in his seat from the adrenaline when I reach for his phone and take it out of his pocket. If he won't tell me what really went down, I'll check myself.

I open the message app and search through his messages until I find Blom's name. They talked a few times, mostly about the cash Blom owed, and this guy not wanting to help him out in any way, even though Blom kept telling him he owed him something.

None of it matters.

Because right there, in the messages, is a current location.

And the following message is Blom telling this guy he's moving hideouts ... but without revealing his location.

Fuck.

I hold the phone so tightly the glass breaks in my hand.

"I need to know where he is now," I say through gritted teeth.

But the man in the chair merely whimpers and shakes his head.

I won't get anything useful out of him.

"Please," the guy mutters as I lift my knife.

But I don't play nice.

And I definitely don't do mercy.

I slice through his neck with no remorse. He oozes blood and gurgles it up, but it doesn't faze me the least bit. He knew there was a price to pay for doing business with Blom and De Vos. This is the consequence of thinking you're too rich to be touched.

After a while, the man slumps in the chair.

I tuck his phone into my pocket along with my knife and then rip off a piece of his shirt, which I use to hold the cut-off finger so it doesn't bleed all over me.

I leave him there and march out the door of his house, where a van is waiting for me. Inside, a woman wails the moment she spots me.

She fights her way out of the hands of my owner's guards and jumps out of the van. "Where's Tom? What did you do with him?"

As I approach her, I hold up the bloody finger, and she begins to weep like a siren, collapsing underneath her own weight.

I go to my knees in front of her and grab her chin so she looks up at me through tearstained eyes. "Tell Blom we have his daughter."

"What?" she mutters as I get up and walk to the van. "But I don't know who that is. My husband never told me wha—"

I close the door before she can say anything else. I'm tired of listening to liars.

Besides, I can't even remotely appear to care.

My owner is always watching.

The van drives off, leaving the woman behind. None of us speak. It's not required. We all know what kind of business we're a part of. Some people play the game and win … others lose.

And I don't intend to be one of them.

My fist tightens.

Whatever it costs me, I will pay the price because freedom is worth it all.

***

When I get back to the mansion, no guards are standing watch. I kick open the office door, only to find my owner discussing with a young, crazy-looking guy with dark hair and a feather earring. I rarely ever see him.

But I know he's my owner's son.

They both look at me like I interrupted an important conversation.

"Oh. Look who's out of his cage," his son, Luca, jests, turning to face me with a smirk on his face. "Beast. Enjoyed your time out?"

I merely grumble and stare.

I've seen Luca only a handful of times when he's come to my cell for a certain occasion. Never as evil as his father to actually set me loose on someone, but definitely fucked up in the head. I could tell that much from the small number of conversations he's had with me.

"What did you make him do?" he asks his father. "Threaten or kill?"

"Neither. Where's that fucker's head?" my owner growls at me.

I throw a tiny package onto his desk, the contents of which bleed all over his papers.

My owner holds up the bloodied finger. "This. This is what you bring me?"

"Blom's location is unknown," I reply.

He smashes the finger down on his desk. "I don't care if it's unknown! That's what you're supposed to find out!"

"Yikes," Luca mutters, rolling his eyes. "You know, I

don't think I'm interested in finding out more about this 'arrangement' you've got going here, Dad," he says, making quotation marks with his fingers. "I have work to do. Talk to you later."

He casually strolls out the door, but not before turning to me and whispering, "Violence tastes the best, don't you think?" He winks and saunters off out the door.

The son is as crazy as his father.

If not crazier.

My owner quickly moves from behind his desk to slam the door shut.

"Blom's messages stopped after he moved hideouts," I say.

"I don't fucking care!" He's shouting so loudly a vein in his eye pops. "I told you to find him for me and bring me his head, and you failed again!"

"Yes, sir," I reply, not even flinching when he comes up and spits in my face.

His teeth grind together as he speaks. "What kind of dog are you if you can't even do a simple fetch?"

I don't respond. I know what I am to him. I've always known. But it doesn't make it any less painful to hear.

My fist tightens as I attempt to control my rage while he circles around me.

Because I know what's about to happen.

What he'll sentence me to.

"Back to your cage, dog," he says. "I will get my men to do your job. Maybe they can teach you something."

Back to my cage.

My hole.

Back to die another day. Slowly but surely.

All because I couldn't make the impossible happen.

A guard comes up from behind me and puts his hand around my neck. My eyes instantly land on the red marks on his finger. Bite marks.

Aurora?

He unlocks the collar from around my neck, releasing me from my shackle, and hands the key back to my owner.

Just as he always does.

The guard pokes at my back with a gun, but one simple growl has him cowering behind me. I walk out of my own free will, back to my cage. Again.

But I know … someday … my time will come.

And when it does, I will rip this house and these people to shreds.

Twelve

Aurora

The second the door at the top of the stairs opens again, I hide in the darkest corner I can find.

Loud, booming steps are audible, followed by smaller ones that I recognize as belonging to Raymond.

I really don't want to see that asshole again. But I'm more concerned about what's coming down the stairs in front of him.

A beast ... with hands covered in blood.

I gulp as Raymond brings him to the cage and opens the door. Raymond throws me a glare as he pushes Beast back inside and shuts the door behind him.

"Have fun with him instead," he sneers at me before returning upstairs.

We're left alone in the dark, but not without a small inkling of light emanating from the top of the stairs. Someone left a light on. Why?

I dare not ask the question out loud.

Especially not with that beastly man staring at me.

And now, with the light on, I can really see all the ridges of his big, flexing muscles, all six of his bulging abs, his giant pecs, and the thick slabs of muscle on his legs and arms. All exquisitely trained to perfection as a predator would.

Maybe Lex was right. Maybe this man does want to devour me whole.

Beast tilts his head, and this minute movement causes my heart rate to shoot up into the sky. Because I know, deep down, I won't be able to fight him off if he does.

But Lex needs me to get my father, right?

If I'm dead, I'm not useful.

Then again, he did say there was a price to pay for not helping him.

I shiver in place.

I wonder where Beast got the bloodied hands. What he had to do. If he did it willingly.

This man is used just like me, but his captivity goes far beyond this cell. The violent things they make him do aren't remotely close to humane. Yet he wasn't dragged back into this cell. He walked in, almost out of his own free will.

He takes off his blood-smeared shirt and throws it in the

corner of the cell.

"Why did you come back?" It's out before I realize it.

He glances at me over his broad shoulders. "I don't have a choice."

I frown. "You could fight your way out, right?"

His eyes narrow. "Don't you think I've tried?"

He turns to face me, and my eyes glide down his chiseled pecs and abs, unable to stop myself. And for some reason, I can picture myself sliding a finger down those very same abs.

Stop.

I shake it off, forcing myself to focus on something else, anything, but it's almost impossible because he takes up so much space in this tiny cell.

I force myself to fixate my attention on the conversation instead of his perfectly carved body. "So Lex keeps you in here and forces you to kill people."

He doesn't respond.

"Is it because of that collar?"

His eyes sharpen almost like a hawk homing in on its prey, and it makes me inch back into the wall.

I almost feel like I should apologize for even asking, but I'm not the bad guy here.

Although, it's almost starting to look like he isn't either.

Which doesn't make any sense. He has blood on his hands. Literally.

"Whose blood is that?" I ask, pointing at his arms.

His eyes lower as his hands rise, and he takes a long

hard look at them as though he hadn't even seen it himself.

But the thought didn't evade me that perhaps they already found my father.

And I'm kept here for the fun of it.

Tears well up in my eyes. "Is it my papa's?"

"No," the man responds, making a fist with his bloodied hands. "I killed his friend."

Another friend … another life lost because of Lex's desire to settle a debt my papa owes.

Horrific. All of it.

"Why?" I mutter. "What did he do to deserve a death like that?"

"To find your father," Beast replies, never evading my eyes.

"And did you?" I ask.

He shakes his head, and my heartbeat finally slows down a little.

"But I will," he adds, his voice chilling.

He steps closer, and for a second, I wonder if he's going to hurt me too. Instead, he pushes a button on the wall right next to me. A shower is turned on mere inches away from me.

I crawl away so I don't get wet, but when I've perched myself in a corner and turn to look, he's already taken off his black cargo pants … and all his other clothes.

My eyes almost drop out of my head at the sight of his sculpted round ass as he steps underneath the shower like it's no big deal. And I can't look away, no matter how hard I try to peel my eyes off him. Every muscle in his body tenses as the blood washes off his hands and disappears down the drain. He grabs a bar of soap lying on a small shelf next to the shower button. With every turn, I catch another glimpse of his abs and thick thighs as he washes them thoroughly. And I still can't manage to look away.

Not until our eyes connect.

And I realize he just caught me staring.

I shut my eyes and wish the blush away, not brave enough to open my eyes again and face the consequences of my actions.

But I don't need to look to know what's happening.

I can hear him turn off the shower. Dry himself off with one of the towels on a rack near the bars. Step closer and closer and closer.

Is he still naked?

I swallow at the thought of seeing his body … and the giant cock dangling between his legs. I've never seen a man before. At least not in real life. I've only seen one on the internet when I was curious.

But I don't think I can avoid it much longer as I can literally hear him breathe.

When I open my eyes, he's right there, hunched in front of me, hands on his knees, the only thing between me and his naked body is the flimsy towel he dried off with.

And it's not long enough to cover the dick dangling between his legs.

Or the tip that's still dripping wet.

Good God.

I swallow away the lump in my throat and quickly look away.

His nostrils flare as he sucks in a breath. "I can smell you."

What the … ?

My cheeks glow even brighter.

Do I stink?

I slowly lean in to my armpits, curious to know what he's talking about, but the scent isn't that bad. Granted, I haven't showered in days. Not that I ever could with the way he's been watching me like a hawk.

But I don't smell what he's smelling.

"Not there," he says, his voice guttural, almost feral like.

He leans in so close he invades my space, and with closed eyes, he takes another whiff, groaning loudly.

And for some reason, it makes my entire body erupt into goose bumps.

No one has ever smelled me before. Not like that.

And definitely not in a way that makes me feel all … tingly.

But he's so close I can't look away, and he keeps inching closer and closer until I have nowhere left to go. I slide down against the wall until I'm flat on the floor with him hovering right above me.

Suddenly, he plants a hand on the concrete ground beside my head. When I try to move sideways, he slams another hand into the floor, trapping me beneath him.

"I'm hungry …" he groans.

How am I going to get out of this one when it's impossible to look away?

Sweat drops roll down my back.

"But you had food this morning," I say, my voice fluctuating in tone.

His lip barely rises as he speaks through his teeth. "I'm hungry for you."

Hungry … for me?

Oh God.

He's not thinking of … actually eating me?

No, no, no, I don't wanna die!

"Please," I mutter, shaking my head, praying he won't kill me too.

His lips part, and his tongue darts out to lick the rim, just like a predator would.

Oh God, Lex was right. This beast does want to eat me.

Sweat drops roll down my neck as I realize this could be the end.

I don't want to die. Not like that. I can't watch.

Instinct makes me close my eyes as he leans in and growls near my ear. "I want to lick you."

My eyes burst open right as his tongue dips out and drags a line down from my ear all the way to my neck. And the groan that follows sets my body on fire.

Getting eaten alive definitely shouldn't be this hot.

His face hovers close to my chin, and I desperately suck in some much-needed air, wondering how many more breaths I'll be able to take before my time is up. I'm shivering and covered in droplets of sweat from fear, wishing this wouldn't be how it all ends, wishing I wasn't frozen in place, completely enamored by this beast of a man as he licks his way down the crevice between my breasts.

My nipples peak, and I whimper from how good it feels when he presses slow, dragged-out kisses all over my chest. But these kisses will only lead to pure terror. I just know it. Any second now, he'll sink his teeth into my flesh and devour me whole.

I gaze down, unable to stop myself from wanting to see it when he starts. With every kiss, I hold my breath, waiting, waiting, but it never comes.

"I don't want …" I can't even finish my sentence because of the way he looks up into my eyes with complete and utter mania, as though he's consumed by the mere idea of eating me.

"You don't want *what*?" he groans. He slides down my dress and grabs my leg, lifting it to his chest, and he throws off my shoes like they're meaningless junk in his way.

And when he presses his lips to my skin, I mutter, "I don't want to die."

Slowly but surely a definite smirk begins to form on his face as he leans up fully, straightening his back until all the individual ridges of his abs are on full display. And even though my eyes are practically glued to his lean body, his penetrative eyes command my attention.

"This won't kill you."

He licks his bottom lip before biting it, which makes my heart throb. Not just in my chest ... but between my legs too.

He grabs my foot and sucks my toe, and I hold my breath, scrunching up my nose, waiting for the bite that doesn't come. His tongue dips out again, dragging a hot, wet line all the way down my knee and thigh, and my entire body begins to zing.

Is he savoring the taste before he has a bite?

I shudder as I think about it, but my thoughts are easily replaced by lust as he dives down between my legs, scrunching up my dress with every kiss he plants. When my panties are exposed, my face turns red.

No one but my maids have ever seen me with just panties on before. Papa always told me no one was allowed to see me without my clothes on, and definitely never without my gloves.

But this man doesn't stop. I don't think he knows the word ... or that he'd ever listen to it.

He spreads my legs farther and farther, and I'm too stunned to provide even the slightest of resistance. His fingers curl around my panties, and without warning, he tears them down.

I gasp in shock, eyes and mouth wide open, while he dives underneath my dress.

"Wha—"

I can't finish my sentence.

Nor do I remember what I was about to say.

Because this man's tongue is right on top of the place I was told never to touch.

**

BEAST

The first lick is the best aphrodisiac in the world.

The mere taste of her is divine, unlike the savory meat my owner would only feed me. No, nothing comes close to the taste of her as I circle her slit and eat her out.

I've never been so hungry in my entire life, and I don't want to wait another second longer. I'm ravenous, dying of a thirst that can only be quenched by tasting the juices that have taunted me since I first smelled her.

God, her scent alone could make me kill.

Hell, I would kill anything in my path to obtain even the slightest lick.

My tongue swivels back and forth, greedy for more. And when I look up, the girl seems too flustered to even speak.

But she doesn't need to say the words out loud for me to know what she's thinking.

I'll eat her up, devour her alive, and leave nothing in my wake.

I can do all of that ... and still, she wouldn't be able to resist.

She's lost all fight that was left in her.

All the pent-up anger was lost the second she laid eyes on my naked body.

I knew it then, and I know it now—she wants me as badly as I want her. And she definitely doesn't need to ask.

"Oh God, what are you doing?" she mutters through heady breaths.

There's no point in explaining it with words when I can let my tongue do the talking.

I lap her up, licking and sucking like my life depends on it. I've eaten many things in my life, but I have never eaten anything that tasted this amazing. I could eat her pussy for days and still not have enough.

I knew it when I licked the salt off her neck that I'd be in for a treat down here.

But the one thing that's managed to subvert my expectation was just how much I enjoy her looking at me while I do this.

Because damn, those caramel eyes, they haunt my very fucking soul.

She immediately closes her eyes and falls back onto the concrete ground.

Too close, too heavy, too hot.

I know the feeling. I know it all too well, but all it does is make me want to get closer, deeper, wetter.

And fuck me, this has been long overdue.

My mouth is on her pussy like I'm eating the best meal I've ever had, and I have no regrets. If someone comes in to watch me feast on her, so be it. I don't have it in me to care. The only thing I want is to lick and suck this pussy raw.

My cock bobs up and down from just the taste, but when she arches her back to meet my lips, that's when it gets hard to maintain control.

Her mewls fill me with uncontrollable lust. I shove my hands underneath her ass to lift her, and I suck on the little swollen clit until she shivers. Goose bumps cover her whole body, and the flush on her skin is a sight to behold.

It's the first time in forever that I'm finally getting a chance to do this again, but I've never had the pleasure of taking a girl who is so eager for more. Most of them begged me to do it in exchange for their life, and I took what I wanted without remorse because I could. Because, in some twisted, sadistic way, I wanted to give those women what they asked for. Their body in exchange for their freedom.

I didn't take them because I wanted to.

But this ... this girl I want.

Badly.

Ferociously.

And I would rather die tomorrow than risk not having buried my tongue in this delicious pussy just to survive. Because damn, I know I'll be punished for doing this, for making her mine, for using her as a toy. I failed my task yet again, so I haven't earned the right to take her.

But she's here now, and I'll be damned if I don't take what's right in front of me while I still can.

I've never felt this before, not for any girl. And the fact

alone that I managed to resist the urge to claim her for so long is a feat in itself. This is pure animalistic thirst, and I've not nearly had enough of her.

I pull her even closer, dragging my lips across her slit until I reach her pussy, and I shove my tongue inside for the real deal. Her mouth forms an o-shape as a hampered moan escapes. She slaps her hand in front of her mouth and looks away, but it only makes me grin harder against her pussy as I thrust in and out, licking her freely flowing juices.

"Beast ..." she mutters.

I've always hated that name. Until she spoke it out loud.

Her voice is like a siren's call to me.

I roll my tongue around her clit and watch her unravel beneath me.

She likes this. Even if she says she doesn't or thinks she shouldn't.

It's all a lie.

And I don't fucking care anymore if she's still scared of me.

I'll show her how good I can make her feel.

With my tongue, I'll teach her how to yield. And when she finally stops fighting, I'll make her mine.

"Oh, no, no, this can't ..." she murmurs, her nails scratching the concrete floor. "You have to stop before I ..."

"I won't," I reply, kissing her clit until her entire body begins to convulse, and when it does, I flick the tip of my tongue along the edge.

She moans out loud, and a gush of wetness flows from her pussy. I lap it all up, the taste divine, just like the look on her face after she just came.

When her clit stops throbbing, I lean up to have a look at her beautifully flushed face. She's breathing so heavily her chest rises and falls, and I can't help but wonder what she'd look like when I tear this dress off her body.

If I should, right now, while she's still warm, wet, and ready for the taking.

The thought of sinking my cock into her velvety pussy makes me salivate as much as licking her did.

But first, I need to make sure she understands.

So I crawl on top of her and press my lips to hers. Tasting her mouth is the icing on top of the cake. Kissing her is as enticing as I remember it being, and my cock twitches from the sheer amount of lust coursing through my veins.

I can't get enough of her.

Until her eyes land on me.

They widen, and she violently jerks away from my lips. She crawls sideways to get out of my hands, shoving down her dress like an angry little bug skittering away in the darkness.

Running away like she has regrets.

Lies.

"That ..." she mutters from her little corner far away from me. "Was not supposed to happen."

My brow rises as I slowly come to a stand. "Then what

was supposed to happen?"

She looks up at me in awe as my towel drops to the floor, her eyes sliding down my body to take it all in. But they stop the second they reach my rock-hard dick. And for a single second, her tongue darts out to wet her lips, only to disappear the next second, as if nothing ever happened.

"Oh God," she says, blocking her own eyes with her hands. "Please put that towel back on."

"Or what?"

She seems on edge. "It's inappropriate."

I tilt my head, amused by this conversation. "Why?"

"I-I don't know!" she yelps. "Just do something."

"I did."

"I … I … not that," she murmurs, still peeking at my body through her fingers.

A smirk forms on my lips. "Not *what*?"

I know she felt it.

I could taste her cum.

Her entire face turns red as a beet. "I thought you were going to eat me."

I wipe my mouth and lick up the remaining juices. "I did."

"Wha-What?" she mutters, her hand slowly lowering as though she can't believe her own ears. She finally realizes what I said, and her face only grows redder. "Oh no. No, that was—"

"Delicious," I reply, my cock oozing pre-cum just from the memory alone.

I'm done waiting around. Her scent drives me insane, and now I want to claim my prize.

But when I step forward, she holds up a hand. She shakes her head, the stunned look on her face quickly being replaced by resentment. "Don't."

First, she pretends not to want me, and now she's angry with me for giving her what we both craved? Strange little creature.

I normally don't stop or listen. Not to anyone but my owner.

But she … she makes me want to do things I've never wanted to do before.

So I stay, grab the towel from the ground, curl it back around my waist, and sit down on the floor to listen.

Thirteen

Aurora

That had to be the best feeling I've ever felt in the whole entire world.

But the problem is, I don't know what the hell he did.

My body is still quaking from the aftermath of his tongue swiveling across my private parts. Just thinking about it makes me glow red and get all hot and bothered, and I don't understand. I've never felt anything like this before, this kind of explosion of lust.

I shiver in place, trying not to freak out, but it's hard with a six-and-a-half-foot naked giant sitting right in front of me. I'm glad he put the towel back on because it'd be impossible to focus on anything other than that huge dick pointing right up at the ceiling.

Good God, it was thick and ... wet.

Even when it's no longer visible, I still can't stop thinking about it.

Maybe I don't want to.

Stop it!

I shake my head.

None of this makes sense. One second, I believe my life is going to end—he's going to eat me, starting with an hors d'oeuvre of my toes—and then the next, he's kissing my legs, my thighs, my ... most sensitive parts.

The parts my papa told me were forbidden.

Not just for me.

Men.

And this Beast *is* a man.

A very rugged, primal, violent kind of man, but a man nonetheless.

And that very same man just licked that forbidden part of me like it was normal. Like it was easy. Like he enjoyed it.

I gulp as he sits there and stares at me as though he's waiting for me to say something. But I don't know what the hell to say. Not to any of this or him.

Because I don't even know what happened.

How he managed to make it feel so damn good.

I shiver, not from fear but from delight, instantly making me hate myself. Every fiber of my being tells me I shouldn't have liked what he did—how he kissed me so gently yet with so much passion, how he licked me like he tasted the world's finest food, how he gave me an explosion of sensations I can only describe as pure and utter ecstasy.

How in the world did he do that?

I don't understand.

And I definitely don't understand how I let this man take what he wanted without putting up a fight.

I should've kicked him off, pushed him, shoved him away.

Instead, I lie down and let him control me, own me, use me, like a meek little lamb ready for slaughter.

I sigh out loud and curl up in my corner, wishing I was alone in this cell so I wouldn't have to face this complicated situation, which just got a whole lot more complicated.

"You despise me," he says.

I can't help but look at him even though I know I shouldn't. Because every time I look at this man, it becomes harder and harder to look away.

"I don't."

"You don't want me close," he says.

"Just because I don't want you close doesn't mean I despise you," I reply.

Maybe he's right. Maybe I do despise him.

But only for making me feel the way he did.

For making me want more of whatever that was.

"I just … don't understand myself right now."

"Why?" he asks.

My face warms up again, remembering him between my

legs and his tongue all over me.

It should be a sin for something to feel that good, yet …

"Because none of that should've happened."

He tilts his head. "Why not?"

"Because it's wrong," I retort.

"Did it feel wrong?" he asks.

The way he looks at me, so completely sincere and without any form of judgment, catches me off guard.

"I …" Now I'm really glowing red. "No, but—"

"Then it wasn't wrong," he interjects.

He's so sincere with his words while I've always tried to erase the truth.

My eyes briefly slide down his towel again, unable to help themselves. I swear, that thing of his just makes it so hard to look away.

Doesn't it hurt him to be that hard? To want someone that badly?

Now I almost feel guilty for stopping him, even when I know in my head it isn't right. But he's still rigid and dripping, almost as if his cock alone is begging for a release that I didn't give.

Oh God, you have to stop thinking about this.

Embarrassed, I look away and hide in my own arms, wishing I could vanish.

"Don't," he says.

I lift my head from my arms, peering at him over my own skin.

"You told me, and I listened … now I'm telling you," he

says, his stare inescapable. "Don't look away."

Don't. I used that word to guard myself.

And he's right. He did stop. But I thought it was just because he was surprised. Not because he actually ... respected me.

"What did you feel when I licked you?" he asks.

I swallow away my own embarrassment. "Like I was a combusting star."

A hint of a smile peaks at his scarred lips. "Have you ever felt it before?"

I shake my head.

The smile only deepens. "It's called an orgasm."

Orgasm. I've read that word. But I've never actually experienced it before.

Just the thought makes me flush with heat again.

It was the best feeling in the entire world, and I definitely understand now why some people would want to kill for this.

"So you've never ... touched yourself?" he asks.

My eyes widen, and I feel all the color instantly drain from my skin. I swiftly shake my head. "I wasn't allowed."

His brow furrows. "By who?"

I avert my eyes. "Papa always said that place was forbidden for anyone but my future husband. Especially for girls like me."

"Girls like you?" Beast scoffs. "What does that mean?"

I don't know why I'm telling him this. I should not be telling anyone this, but especially not the man who brought me into this cell to begin with.

God, what am I doing?

"Nothing," I mutter, hoping he'll forget.

I quickly get up and start searching this cell, not giving a shit that Beast is still sitting in the middle, staring at me wherever I go. I ignore his hawk-like gaze and focus on the bars and all the nooks and crannies.

I search every corner, and nothing is left untouched. I have to find something, anything, to get out of here. Maybe there's a crack, a broken bar, a small stone missing from the walls. Who knows. All I know is that I should've done this sooner.

"What are you doing?" he suddenly asks.

"Trying to find a way out of here," I respond.

"There isn't any. I've tried," he replies.

I pause and glance at him over my shoulder. "What if you're lying?"

"I don't lie," he retorts.

"Well, you did," I scoff, rolling my eyes.

"When?" he growls, his voice darker than before.

But I can't tell him when because then I have to blush again, and I hate that. I hate that he continuously makes me blush because I've never felt my face flush this many times in my life.

"When you said you didn't want to take my body as payment," I say.

I can't even look at him when I say it.

"I wanted you." Without hesitation. Zero. And it makes

me pause. "But *he* was watching."

I glance at him over my shoulder. "What do you mean?"

He taps his neck. "The collar."

I gasp. "It contains a camera?"

He nods.

Good god, what kind of psychotic man do you have to be to put not only a collar around someone else's neck but to also track them and put a camera in it as well? Just to keep track of everything he does?

I sigh. "No wonder you call him *owner*. You have to do what he tells you, or he punishes you. And there's no way to hide. No lying. He can see everything you do." After a while, I finally gather the courage to step closer to him, and I point at my face right where his scars are. "Did Lex give those to you?"

Beast nods, but his face darkens, and he looks away. "A price to pay for my failure."

"Your owner is a cruel man," I say. "You must know that, right?"

He gets up from the floor, adjusting his towel as it loosened up from his stature alone. "What I know or feel doesn't matter."

"Yes, it does," I reply, clutching the bars. "They shouldn't treat you like this." When I turn to look at him, he just stands there, arms folded, leaning against the wall. "Why did you stop fighting?"

He points at his neck. "The collar."

"Does it hurt when it's on?"

He nods. "Electricity."

My pupils dilate. "Oh wow. They actually electrocute you? Constantly?"

He shakes his head. "My owner has a button."

I didn't know it went that far, but the savagery of Lex really knows no bounds.

"No wonder you never rebel," I say, turning to face him. "Is that why you brought me to him instead of letting me go?"

He nods.

It's silent for a moment, but my brain keeps churning. That collar was the whole reason he almost choked me, brought me to that hotel, kept me like a captive, and dragged me back here. He didn't have a choice, even if he wanted to.

He's as much a prisoner to this place as I am.

And maybe, just maybe, keeping him on my side isn't merely a matter of survival. It could mean my only ticket to freedom.

Suddenly, the door at the top of the stairs opens again. Neither of us moves a muscle as we stare at each other. At that moment, it feels almost as if I understand him, if only just a little. But that small inch of mutual understanding is enough to fuel a spark of rebellion in my heart.

The steps that pounce down the stairs are slow and heavy, and when I turn to look, a chill runs down my spine.

Lex is smiling in such a devilish manner that I'm not sure I can stop myself from heaving.

"You two … I heard from the guards upstairs you were having fun," he says. "Is that true?"

Fun?

The word alone makes bile rise in my throat.

"I-I don't know wha—"

"Nonsense, girl." He steps closer, not close enough for me to reach him through the bars but close enough for him to show me who's in control. "I trust my guards. They know what they heard."

My entire face begins to glow.

"See?" he muses, smiling even harder until it suddenly disappears. "I didn't give you permission, Beast," he spits at the man in the cell with me.

Raymond comes down the steps too now, carefully assessing the situation while Lex moves to the door.

"You, with me," he tells me as he opens it up. "You, stay," he growls at Beast.

But Beast merely snarls at him, grinding his teeth.

Lex beckons me to come. "Come here. Now."

I shake my head. "No."

Suddenly, he pulls out a stun gun. "You want me to use this on you?" he growls, pointing it dangerously close to me. "Because I will."

Beast pushes himself off the wall, broadening his shoulders.

CLICK!

The sound of the safety being pulled off a gun doesn't go unnoticed. Both Beast and I freeze, my pulse quickening as Raymond points his gun at Beast's head.

"Don't. Move."

Beast's face contorts, but he remains put where he was, watching like a hawk as I slowly move away from the bars and into Lex's hands.

The feel of his grip around my waist as he pulls me out of the cage makes my insides knot.

"I'll take her now," he tells Beast with a filthy grin. "You won't mind if I borrow your toy for a while, will you?"

Beast merely growls, but his eyes are filled with a fire I've only ever seen once before; when I tried to shoot him.

"Thought so," Lex adds, and he quickly removes me from the cage before shutting the door behind us, sealing it tight. "It's about time we had another chat."

Fourteen

BEAST

Raymond walks to the back of the cellar and fetches some fresh clothes, which he throws at me through the bars. "Put some clothes on, you bastard."

I ignore his words.

"Where did he take her?" I growl.

He just smirks at me. "Who the fuck knows. Why do you care so badly? Got a little crush, doggy?"

I slam the bars with my bare hands. "Give her back!"

He laughs and steps even closer, dangling the keys between his fingers like he's taunting me with true freedom nearly within my reach. "You think she's yours?"

"My owner gave her to me," I say through gritted teeth. "Where is she?"

"If I had to guess …" He licks his lips. "The bedroom."

I shove myself into the bars and lunge through them with a single arm, grasping ahold of his shirt and dragging him toward me. "If any of you hurt her, I'll fucking eat you alive."

The guy's pupils dilate, and he quickly pulls out the stun gun and rams it into my chest.

I groan out loud from the sheer pain of the electrical current coursing through my veins.

"Get your filthy fucking hands off me," Raymond growls.

He applies another pulse, forcing me to release him.

He swiftly steps away, out of my reach, while I catch my breath with my hands on my knees, breathing through the pain.

With a foul grimace on his face, he says, "You fucking try any of that shit on me again, and I will fucking shoot you."

"You're not allowed," I say, gazing up from underneath my eyelashes. "I'm far too valuable to him."

He sneers, "I'll fucking blast you with this stun gun all fucking day if you keep it up."

I don't relent. "Bring. Her. Back."

"Just because you had some fun with your shiny little toy doesn't make her yours," he replies, straightening his shirt. "Don't you forget who owns you."

My nostrils flare. "Mark my words. If he hurts her, I will slaughter each and every one of you."

His eyes widen, and he steps away while I stare until he's gone back up the stairs and locked the door, sealing me away in the darkness.

But we both know no amount of wood or steel can ever contain this beast.

One fucking day …

I will rain down hell.

***

AURORA

Up the stairs, the light takes some adjusting. I blink a couple of times, but the door closing behind me makes me jolt.

Lex laughs and continues his walk, flicking his finger, and I take it as a sign to follow him. He's definitely shown me what he's capable of, and I don't think I want to find out what he'll do to me if I don't listen.

I gulp as he brings me into a giant hallway and goes up the stairs. I silently traipse behind him, gazing around to take in my environment in case I'll ever need to tell the cops, or my father's men, about this place.

A big chandelier hangs from the ceiling, extravagant paintings of beautiful women and scenery all around, carpets on the floor that look handmade, and a few intricately painted vases. The man is rich, that much is certain, but the price it cost was heavy.

My hand slips on the banister, and I raise my fingers only to see caked blood.

I gasp.

Lex pauses and glances at me over his shoulder, his eyes quickly trailing down to my hand. "Oh. Seems the maid forgot to clean that spot."

My stomach almost turns around right there and then, but I swallow back down the panic and wipe my fingers on my already bloodied dress. Then I throw him an awkward smile.

"But you're used to seeing blood, right?" he bemuses.

Like it's the most normal thing in the world.

"Your father wasn't exactly a proper tradesman, now was he?"

I simply nod.

"We all do things we're not proud of. For the greater good," he adds, and he turns around and marches off.

I quickly follow him into a room up ahead filled with expensive-looking furniture—thick, red curtains in front of huge panel windows, a leather lounge in the middle, a black piano in the back, and a bed with soft pillows that I could drown in. If I could stay here instead, maybe it wouldn't be so difficult to be a prisoner.

But the sound of a door closing behind me evaporates that thought.

"This is my wife's room. She's gone for the moment. Business trip to Germany," Lex says. "She has to fix the mess my sons left behind." He snorts as if it's some funny inside joke that I'm not privy to.

Lex opens the closet to the left and grabs a bright-blue dress, holding it up. "Put this on."

I frown. "What, now?"

He sneers, "Yes, now."

My eyes skid back and forth between this room and the closet, wondering if he's for real or if he's joking. I can't take off my clothes right here, right now, not with him looking.

But he looks dead serious.

And I'm not in the position to refuse him.

I approach him slowly and snatch the dress from his snake hands, making sure there's ample room between us. I wait, but he keeps standing there, gazing at me like he wants me to do it in front of him.

"Can I at least have some privacy?" I ask.

He sighs out loud. "Fine." He walks past me and out of the closet. "But if you're not out in five, I'll come in and get you myself."

I nod and quickly close the door so I can breathe. Just for a moment. Just breathe.

When I've calmed down, I kick off my shoes, slide down my panties, and steal a fresh pair from the closet. I'm surprised by how well they fit when I put them on. But the dress is so tight I can barely zip it up. My breasts almost spill out, and my waist is cinched so harshly I can't breathe normally.

A knock on the door makes me jolt. "Are you coming out or not?"

"In a second," I reply.

I quickly put on my shoes again, wanting to keep at least one remnant of myself with me as I step out of the closet. Lex looks at me, his eyes sliding up and down my body like he's rating me. And it makes me feel like a pet getting a mark at a judging competition.

"Beautiful," he says. "Just like my wife, Anne."

A creepy smile forms on his lips, making me nauseous.

Why do I have this feeling he's dressing me up like a doll?

He walks past me to the piano and presses a key. "Anne used to play this all the time back when she was younger." He glances at me over his shoulder. "I'm told you do too?"

I suck in a breath. "For my papa, yes."

"He had you play professionally?"

I nod.

He moves to the side of the piano and points at the bench. "Show me."

My heartbeat is going haywire as I walk closer and sit down. I place my hands on the keys, gazing up at Lex before I begin to play, just as I was taught.

My hands glide across the piano, and I close my eyes and sink into the music like I always do, pretending I'm somewhere in a faraway land with the sun shining on my skin and a heavenly breeze wafting through my hair.

But the image is disturbed by Lex moving to the lounge

and sitting down in silence. I feel watched.

Suddenly, he coughs, and when I briefly steal a glance, he holds a napkin in his hand that's covered in blood.

Is he … sick?

Despite being distracted, I continue to play as best as I can.

"Do you always play with gloves on?"

I hit a false note, the sound making me cringe.

"Yes," I answer.

"Pity. I think you'd do much better if you took them off."

I grasp my gloves and touch the embroidered rose. These used to give me so much comfort and made me feel protected. But now? Now all they do is remind me of my papa, who isn't here to protect me.

***

Past, age 8

I grab my diary and write down the words I've written every day since my mother brought me into this world.

Please let me go to school. Please let me go to school!

It's always been a dream of mine, but my papa never let me go. Just like it's been my dream to go to the beach, an amusement park, or the mall. Things normal kids see and do. Kids who don't have an overprotective papa.

I have many dreams, and this diary is the only place I can ever write about them without my papa finding out. Because if he did, he'd probably scold me for even having them.

I finish with hearts and close the diary, pushing it far underneath my bed where it'll stay until the next time I open it.

I hop off the bed and go downstairs with a big smile, and I greet the guards and our help along the way.

"Good morning!" I chant.

"Well, good morning to you too, Little Miss Chipper," one of the maids muses with a grin. "Hope you have a great day!"

"Thank you," I say, and I hug her tight before I head into the living room, where Papa is already enjoying his morning coffee in his chair.

"Good morning, Papa," I say, hopping toward him to give him a kiss on the cheek.

"Good morning, Aurora," he replies. "Have you showered already? You're normally never this quick."

"I know, but I was too excited," I say, sitting on the couch in front of him. "It's a special day today."

"Oh, is it?" He turns the page of his newspaper, seemingly oblivious to my cheerful smile.

"Of course, don't be silly," I reply, playing along.

"Hmm … what for? I wonder," he says, casually taking a sip of his coffee.

And now I'm beginning to wonder if he'll ever notice at all.

"You don't remember?" I ask.

He looks up from his coffee. "Remember what?"

All the warmth leaves my face, and my smile disappears. "Well, it's-it's …"

"It's what?" he says, putting down his newspaper as well as his coffee cup. "Speak clear sentences."

"Yes, of course. Sorry, Papa." I swallow away my pride. "I meant, it's my … birthday."

He tilts his head, his eyes homing in on mine.

Suddenly, he leans forward and pulls a tiny package from behind his back.

My eyes widen at the sight of a beautifully wrapped gift, and I light up like the fireworks I so often view from my window. "Is that for me?"

"Who else do you think it's for?" He laughs as he places the gift on my lap.

So he didn't forget after all. He was just playing with me. I breathe a sigh of relief.

"Well, go on then. Unwrap it," he says.

Not another second do I wait before I tear off the wrappings and pretty bow. Beneath it is a small blue box, and when I pull up the lid, a pair of white gloves are inside with a rose embroidered on top.

"What do you think?" Papa asks as I hold them up to look at them. "Do you like them?"

I nod, but I don't really know what to think. Why did he

give these to me?

"Go on then. Put them on," he says.

I do what he asks, and the material feels quite soft to the touch.

"I had them custom made for you," he adds.

"Thank you," I mutter, still admiring how good they look on my hands. I splay my fingers, and to my surprise, everything looks … gorgeous.

"Check the box," he says.

Wait, did I forget something?

I peer inside and find a letter on the bottom. I open it up and read it.

It's an acceptance letter to the English school here in the Netherlands. The school where all the English kids and expats go after they've moved here. And it's the one school I was begging my papa to let me go to all this time.

I squeal and jump up and down in sheer delight. "Thank you, Papa!" I run to him and fall into his arms, hugging him tight.

He chuckles and awkwardly coughs. "Yes, yes, you're welcome, but enough hugs."

I pull away quickly. "Sorry, Papa. I just got so excited." I rub my lips together and hold the paper tightly against my chest. "This means so much to me. Much more than those gloves ever could."

"Well, you'd better like them because you're not going there unless you wear them," he says.

I stare down at my gloved hands.

"Every single day," he says. "The second you step foot outside or when there are guests in our house."

The joyful smile on my face slowly vanishes with every word he utters.

"Do you want to go to that school?" he asks.

I nod. It's the one thing I've wanted for most of my life; to be a normal kid.

He stands up and caresses my cheek with the back of his hand. "Then you'll wear the gloves like an actual proper lady."

He presses a kiss to my forehead, something he rarely, if ever, does.

"Think of it this way. These gloves are a symbol of my trust in you. And if you wear these," he murmurs, gazing into my eyes. "I will always be there to watch over you."

***

Present

I bite my tongue to stop myself from speaking. When I gaze up at Lex, he pats the lounge while gazing at me.

I swallow back the lump in my throat and slowly make my way over to him, sitting down as far away from him as I possibly can. But he still scoots closer. "Don't worry … it's just the two of us."

Suddenly, he places his hand on my knee.

I freeze.

"Your guards are still in the house," I say.

"They won't interrupt."

Oh God.

What does he intend to do with me?

"You know, I'm quite disappointed in the way Beast handled things. If it was up to me, your father would've long been dealt with." He squeezes my knee. "And you wouldn't be in this precarious position."

I swallow away the lump in my throat.

"Sitting in that cell with little food, water, clothes…" he says, eyeing me, "with that beast … it must've done a number on you."

"I'm fine," I mutter, but my voice comes out in a squeak.

"You don't look fine," he says. "In fact, what I heard from my guards was that Beast already had his way with you. Is that true?"

Sweat drops roll down my back, but I try to stay calm even though, on the inside, I want to scream just because of his fingers slowly creeping upward across my leg.

"You know, he didn't do his job very well, but maybe now that he's had his fill, he'll finally do what needs to be done," he says.

I feel like my throat is clamping shut, stopping me from breathing.

"And I believe you can be of use to me too. I need to take the edge off things."

His hand slides to his crotch.

Bile rises in my throat.

He zips down. "You know what to do, girl."

My entire body quakes as tears form in my eyes. "No."

"No?" His brow rises. "You think you have a choice?" He grabs my chin and makes me look at him. "I think you owe me payment for keeping you alive."

He tries to push my head down, but the thought of doing anything with that man makes me want to vomit.

I thought I could do this, that I could be the good girl my papa always envisioned and be on his side forever. But I can't do this anymore. I can't be the sacrifice my father wants me to be.

I use all of my remaining energy to stand and step away from the lounge. "I'll help you find my father." Lex's eyes begin to glimmer. "That's what you want, isn't it?"

A smile forms on his face. "And how do you think you can help me?"

"He'll listen to me," I say, hovering near the door as Lex stands. "I can call him, his friends, his partners. I know you want his money more than you want his life."

Lex's eyes narrow. "Go on."

"Papa has a secret account. He doesn't use it often, but I know where he keeps the files. And if you can find him, I can make him tell me the PIN. He may not tell you, but he'll tell me because he wants me safe."

A humming sound comes from his throat.

"You're as cunning as your father, it seems," he says. "Good girl."

A chill runs up and down my spine.

I know what I just committed to.

But there's no going back now.

"When I find your father, you will talk to him and make him give me the money he owes me …" he says, cracking his knuckles without moving an inch. "Or your body—your life—will be mine."

Fifteen

BEAST

When the door opens again and I hear the familiar soft steps of the girl, I jump at the cage and cling on for dear life, trying to get as close as I possibly can to see her walk down the stairs.

She's wearing a long, blue dress that barely fits her. But her eyes are wild, and that face ... she looks like she's seen a ghost.

Raymond pushes her down and opens the cage while keeping one hand on the stun gun, ready to strike at me if needed. He shoves her inside and shuts the door as quickly as he can before I even have a chance to pounce on him.

I growl out loud at Raymond as he turns and walks up the stairs again, leaving us alone. A tiny light is switched on in the back of the cell, just like before when I needed a shower.

Most of the time, the lights are off, but when it's on, it's a small slice of heaven.

Except when it isn't.

Because the look on her face is anything but heavenly.

She shivers all over, and when I try to approach her, she jolts back in a knee-jerk reaction. "Don't."

My fists tighten. "Did he hurt you?"

Her eyes flash up to mine. One moment, she nods, then she shakes her head.

"Which is it? Yes or no?" I ask.

"He tried," she says, hiccupping as a single tear rolls down her cheeks. "But I sold out my own father to make it stop."

Sold out her own father?

To make what stop?

Did he fucking touch her?

Just the thought of him putting his filthy hands on her makes me seethe with rage.

She looks down at herself, the panic in her eyes growing. "Oh God."

Her hands reach behind her back, and she immediately unzips the dress. It spills over her breasts, but she holds on tight, blushing crazily. "I have to get it off. Please. I need this thing off me!"

Her voice is as erratic as her behavior, and I struggle to understand what to do with it. But when I approach her again, she inches back.

"I need this to be off. Now," she mutters.

I nod and walk to the back of the cell, turning around to give her some privacy.

I hear her throw it off and chuck it into a corner, her teeth clattering. So I turn on the shower from where I'm at and look at her shadow dancing on the wall.

"Can you stay like that? Turned away?"

I nod. "If that's what you want."

She breathes out a sigh of relief, and I hear more stuff coming off. All of it is chucked to my right, and I can see the stack growing. A dress, shoes, panties, and a bra.

"What did he do to you?" I ask, wondering what it would take for someone to want to undress so violently.

"He made me put that thing on," she says. "To make me look like his wife."

Fuck.

What a fucking bastard.

"Did he hurt you?" I ask, making a fist, ready to punch a hole into this wall as well as that fucker. "Because if he did, I swear I'll—"

Something soft and velvety is slipped off and thrown into the corner to my right. Gloves. "You'll do what?"

I'll kill him.

Cut off his limbs.

Poke out his eyes.

Make him eat his own dick.

But I realize now that's only a fantasy. In this prison, I am nothing but a caged beast with unrelenting hatred and fury.

And he knows this.

She knows this.

"I want to protect you," I say.

It's quiet for a moment, and I wish I could look at her. It's costing every inch of my self-control not to.

"I can protect myself," she replies.

It's practically silent around me until her body finally interrupts the water clashing down onto the ground.

For a single second, I catch a glimpse of her soft skin through the reflection of the mirror near the sink, and our eyes connect.

"Please, don't look at me."

My eyes avert back to the wall as puffs of steam blow past me and onto the wall, allowing me to paint a picture with water of what I saw in that single moment.

It's beautiful.

"Why are you scared?" I ask.

"I'm not," she says. "It's just …" She sighs. "Forget it."

"No," I say. "I want to know."

"My father told me it was forbidden," she says.

Forbidden.

Seems he used that word a lot.

"He doesn't own you," I say. "Not the way my owner owns me."

She doesn't respond. But I know she heard me.

Footsteps are audible, and the shower is turned off. She grabs the last towel off the shelf and I can hear her swaddle herself.

I glance at her pile of clothes, which remains untouched.

"I don't want to put it back on," she murmurs, "but I have nothing else."

I immediately take off the long white shirt the guard chucked at me and throw it over my shoulder without a second thought. "You can have mine."

***

AURORA

First, he offers to protect me.

Now he offers me his clothes?

I'm too flabbergasted to say anything, let alone move. Even though he stays put near the wall, dangling that shirt of his like it's a peace offering.

I thought I was confused before, but now ...

Sighing, I step closer and quickly grasp the shirt, putting it on before he can see me naked. Then I sneak over to the pile of clothes and grab the gloves, tucking my hands inside. The panties I stole are still good, so I put those on too.

I don't have any leggings in here, but his shirt is long enough to cover me like a dress.

When I look down to check, my nostrils catch a whiff of his scent. My cheeks flush as endorphins rush through my body.

No one's ever been this kind to me before, yet he's the reason I'm in here in the first place.

All of these conflicting emotions are hard to swallow.

"I'm dressed now," I say.

He briefly glances at me over his shoulder before turning around. The grumpy look on his face makes me feel confused.

"What?" I immediately look down at the gloves, but they're on correctly so that can't be it.

Only when I look up do I notice the extra wound on his belly. My eyes widen in shock. "Who did that to you?"

"Raymond," he replies, taking in a big breath.

I grimace. "Why? What happened?"

I shouldn't care, but for some reason, I do.

But when his fists tighten and his jaw clenches, I realize there can only be one reason.

My eyes widen. "Because of me?"

He nods, and my stomach drops.

"I like you."

What?

No, that can't be true.

I shake my head. "Don't say that."

Even if it is true, I do not want him to bear these scars.

Not for me. Not for anyone, but definitely not for me.

I shake my head. "You brought me here." It's impossible to hold back the anger lacing my voice. "It's because of you that I'm in this cell, this prison."

The look in his eyes is full of pain, and it hurts. It physically hurts.

No one should feel this way.

And he should definitely not feel that way about me.

He's my captor.

The one I should hate.

And now he goes around saying he *likes* me?

His free hand rises to my face and cups my cheek, and I hold my breath as he brushes away the single tear rolling down. "Why are you crying?"

"Because you said you like me … but no one should ever like me," I say.

He grimaces and shakes his head. "Why?"

More tears tumble down, but he catches them all as if on a mission to stop me from feeling sad. "Because I'm about to help this man catch my own papa."

"It's okay," he says, leaning in until his forehead is on mine.

I try to shake my head, but it's impossible when he looks at me like that. He's so close, I can feel his breath against my lips, taunting me to inch closer.

"What kind of daughter betrays her own father?" I mutter.

"The kind that wants to live," he says.

Is it really that simple?

His eyes are mesmerizing up close, like tiny stars in a galaxy I could float away in.

And for a second, I almost forget we're captives in a cell.

"I don't want to hurt you," he growls with such a low tone it makes goose bumps scatter on my skin. "But I *crave* you."

My breath falters.

His voice grows darker with every word. "I've never craved anyone."

Good God.

My eyes close as he leans in farther and presses the softest of kisses to my lips. He's so gentle it almost feels as though he views me as some kind of flower he doesn't want to damage.

And it moves me.

I don't fight, and I don't push him away. I let him kiss me, again and again, the little pecks of desire making me want to arch my back and fall into his arms.

Even though he could easily take me, use me, do with me whatever he wanted to, he's held back all this time.

It's like he's a complete savage who's unaware of the power he holds. Someone who's never known love or comfort. Like he's been deprived of everything that makes a person human. Yet at the same time, he's the most human person in this house.

When his lips briefly release mine, my body is filled with

warmth and something else … longing.

His eyes bore into mine, the tension between us feeling like it could set this whole house ablaze.

"I want to kiss you, touch you, lick you," he whispers. "Bury my cock inside your pussy and fill you to the brim with my seed."

Oh my God.

His dirty words make my clit thump, and the feeling is so unfamiliar that I clamp my legs together.

It isn't right. None of this is.

Yet I find myself hovering closer and closer to him as he snakes his hand up and down my arm, leaving heat wherever he goes.

His mouth is on mine again, and every kiss is followed by a moan as if he's struggling to contain himself, and for some reason, it makes me want to get closer. So close I can feel his body against mine, all the hard ridges of his abs and the big bulge hardening in his pants.

I don't know if I believe his words, but I believe his body, and it definitely wants me.

So much that I begin to wonder … What if I could make him trust me?

If I could show him what it means to care for another, the meaning of love, he could be on my side. And if I have this savage on my side … I could have a chance at escaping this hellhole.

All I have to do is the one thing I tried to offer him before. Myself.

Sixteen

BEAST

There is nothing on this earth I have wanted more than freedom ... until her.

My hand snakes around her waist as I pull her close, probing her mouth with my lips until I break through, and I lick the roof of her mouth until she gasps. I moan into her mouth and circle her tongue, grasping her ass and squeezing tightly.

I can't control myself any longer.

I tried. I fucking tried so hard.

But something about this attraction is visceral, this need I feel to own her completely. And fuck me, I can't stop myself any longer. I don't want to anymore.

I want to show her how good it can feel, make her yield with just my tongue.

So I drag my lips all along her neck and down to her collarbone, pressing kisses along the way, sending her into a spiral of heat. I can feel it on her skin, the excitement, the desire. It's the same kind I've felt ever since I laid eyes on her, ever since I put my hands on her.

With one hand, I cup her ass while the other snakes its way underneath her shirt. My shirt. The shirt that now smells like both her and me, and it's an intoxicating mix that gets me fucking high with lust.

She shudders as I reach up her belly, my fingers sliding along her soft skin. When I reach her tit, she gasps, but I cover her mouth with mine to silence her.

I don't want those guards up there to hear us.

I don't want to give them a reason to come down and interrupt us.

And I definitely don't want to give anyone an opportunity to come and take her away from me.

She's mine, and every fiber in my body urges me to show her.

So I don't stop as my fingers cross her nipples, circling the tip until her cheeks flush with redness.

"Oh God …"

I grin against her lips. "First a beast, now a god."

Her eyes widen, and she suddenly pulls away from my grasp.

But I won't let her run away. Not this time.

I stalk after her as she walks back until she bumps into the wall. I'm right there to catch her, planting my hands right beside her head. "Don't run away from me," I growl.

She gulps, eyeing my bare, muscled chest. "I'm scared."

I reach for her face and caress her cheek. "I won't break you."

But she places a hand on my abs, which tighten underneath her touch as she pushes.

My cock is almost bursting out of my pants, and waiting like this demands a kind of patience I've never known. And when her hand slips down every ridge, it bobs up and down in my cargo pants.

But nothing could've prepared me for the thrill that comes with her going to her knees right in front of me.

Her hands are on my waist, sliding farther and farther, peeling down my pants until my cock pops out and the pants drop down onto the floor.

She swallows, visibly shaken by the size.

Beautiful, soul-crushing eyes on me.

She seems hesitant but still leans in.

***

Aurora

I'm shaking with nerves, wondering if I can do this.

He's huge, and I've never done this before, yet my pussy throbs at the thought.

If I can please him… maybe he'll help me.

I lean in and open my mouth.

The first lick is nothing like I expected it to be. Salty and hot. Tantalizing.

Only one lick and his entire body grows rigid, cock bobbing up and down against the tip of my tongue.

And for some reason, it makes me feel … powerful.

He groans out loud as I lick the tip again, and I'm wondering how far I'm willing to go.

But I'm already down on my knees, right in front of this man and his giant cock.

There is no way back from here.

He wants me.

He's made that very clear.

And if I don't give him what he wants, I don't think he'd be able to contain it much longer.

The lust in his eyes grows with every lick as I slide my tongue up and down his shaft slowly, taking my time to get used to the feeling.

I've never done this before, and now my first time will be in captivity. But I had to do something to quell Beast's thirst.

He's wanted to take me since he laid eyes on me, and I could feel from the way he kissed me he wanted to own me.

Completely.

And it scared me.

But what scares me the most is just how much I enjoy the look on his face as I kiss the most sensitive part of his body. Something is insanely mesmerizing about watching a man slowly unravel because of your mouth. And also insanely immoral.

I knew I had to do something to temper his desires, and this was the only thing I could think of. Licking him … the way he licked me.

But I never expected it to actually make my own pussy throb too.

I swallow away the lust building deep inside me and focus on pleasuring him instead.

I know it's wrong. I know I shouldn't be doing this.

But I also know doing this could make him want to protect me and help me get out of here. That's why I'm doing it. At least, that's what I tell myself as I lick up and down his length, watching goose bumps erupt all over his body.

He groans out loud as his cock bobs up and down against my mouth, and I revel in delight.

I can't help but look up and watch in awe of this man, this powerful beast who could snap a person in half with ease, knowing I am the one who can make him quiver.

I roll my tongue over his base and move to the tip, which oozes pre-cum. It tastes so salty, but at the same time, it's such a turn-on, and I find myself forgetting more and more about who I am and where I am, consumed by the heat of the moment.

His hand rises to meet my face, and he caresses me gently, his grip tightening around my chin as though he struggles to keep himself from forcing me over his entire length.

"I want to feel your tongue," he groans, his finger lingering on my lips as he lowers my jaw even farther than before.

The thought alone gets me going, and I let him guide me over his cock, pushing myself farther and farther until I gag.

I pull back only to continue licking, but he can't stop pushing inside farther and farther, and I'm not even sure I mind losing control. In fact, it only makes my pussy clench harder.

For some reason, despite knowing exactly what this man did to me, I still want to give him pleasure. And I can't stop gazing up into those eyes that could destroy me in a flash.

I never imagined any of this to be so … sexy.

Or that I'd ever enjoy it as much as I do.

With every thrust, he goes farther and farther, his fingers squeezing my jaw as he slowly loses control. I can see it in his eyes, the animalistic need to ravage, and it's an overpowering feeling.

I've never wanted to give anyone, let alone a man of this size, my body or my mouth, yet here I am offering it to him freely.

It's just to get him on your side. To make him help you break out of here.

But no matter how many times my brain tries to tell me

this, I can't stop my pussy from throbbing harder and harder with each thrust into my mouth.

I have no clue what I'm doing, but he *knows*.

He knows so well how to use my tongue to his advantage, how to push without going too far, how to chip off tiny pieces of my defense without breaking me.

But the way he looks at me, so deeply possessive, that's what will ultimately break me.

And I can't even look away. No matter how hard I try.

Not even as he buries himself inside me to the base.

Tears well up in my eyes, and his other hand brushes them away as they roll down my cheeks.

"Don't cry, beauty."

What did he just call me?

"Take it like a good girl."

My pupils dilate, but I can't pull away. Not with him lodged this deep inside me.

And I'm not even sure I want to because those words alone made me wet.

He keeps going, each thrust more relentless than the other, until I have no choice but to sit back and let him take over.

His fingers slide down and clasp my throat as he uses my mouth to pleasure himself.

His groans are loud and sound more like that of a wolf than a man as he buries himself inside, and I struggle not to heave. He's huge, overpowering, and I'm completely at his mercy.

All my thoughts have gone out the window as I'm consumed by this man, this beast who calls me a beauty when no one else ever would.

He doesn't know.

I blink a couple of times, but the thought disappears as quickly as it came because he buries himself so deep inside me my eyes almost roll into the back of my head.

"I want to fill up your pretty mouth," he says.

But I can't utter a single word, not even if I tried.

The thought of him coming inside me frightens me, but at the same time, I want to find out what it feels like. What it tastes like.

He groans loudly, the salty pre-cum slathering all over my tongue. He feels huge inside me, and I can't help but feel overwhelmed. With his hand around my throat, I'm at his mercy.

"Look at me," he rasps, and my eyes shoot up to his.

He's going so deep I can barely keep up, and I struggle to breathe through it.

But my pussy … God, it throbs with an unquenchable thirst.

And it confuses me so much that I just let it all happen as he sinks deep inside my throat, my saliva spreading all over his length and dripping down onto the concrete floor.

I'm lost in his darkened eyes, enraptured by the way he uses me to his heart's content.

Suddenly, he howls and buries himself to the base, and my eyes widen the second I feel a warm jet of cum shoot down my throat. It's salty and so much that I struggle to swallow it, as most of it drips out of my mouth and onto the concrete. But he doesn't seem to take notice as he keeps on emptying himself inside me, filling me with every last drop.

It's almost as if he saved it all for me.

A final groan and he pulls out his half-hard cock, making me cough and heave.

The rest of his cum drips down my lips, and I lick it up, the salty taste not as bad as I imagined it to be. It's actually quite enticing.

So much that my pussy throbs again, and my cheeks turn strawberry red.

"You look so good with my cum in your mouth," he says with a low voice, making me feel even more self-conscious about the fact that this man's dick was just in my mouth.

His free hand rises to my face, and his thumb swipes across my lip, pushing in the remaining cum and pressing down on my tongue until I suck it off. The most delectable groan rumbles from deep within his chest.

His hand clenches around my throat, and I hold my breath as he lifts me from the ground with ease.

I claw at his fingers, my pupils dilating as I struggle to even breathe.

Is this the end? Did I misjudge the situation?

"I gave you what you wanted," I mutter with exasperation. "Don't kill me."

"Kill you?" His brow rises, and his fingers stop digging

into my skin, allowing me to gulp in some much-needed oxygen.

He pushes me against the wall and leans in, whispering into my ear, "I could *never* kill the girl I desire."

Seventeen

BEAST

The second she went down on her knees, I knew I wouldn't be able to resist.

And now look at the mess I made.

Keeping her pinned to the wall, I lean in and press my lips to hers, tasting my own seed on her lips, and I don't give a fuck. All I want is for her to know just how much I want her ... how much I need her to be mine.

I groan against her lips, biting and tugging on the bottom one, then mutter, "Delicious."

With her eyes closed and that pink flush on her face, she looks just like a doll I ravaged. But I need her to know I don't want to break what's left of this beautiful doll.

I want her to feel what I've been feeling since I first met her. I want her to feel just as good as I did when her tongue wrapped around my cock. Because when I buried myself inside her throat, it was nothing short of pure ecstasy.

And now it's her turn.

My hand slowly unravels from around her neck, only to slide down her chest between her tits. With my other hand splayed firmly against the wall behind her, I lean in to look into her eyes as I slowly make my way down her body with the gentlest of touches. Everywhere my hand goes, her body tenses, and her breathing falters, but my eyes never leave hers.

I want her to look at me as I touch every inch of her body and make it mine.

My fingers briefly skim her nipples, and they grow taut almost immediately, making me groan with delight.

"When I touched you, you tried to run," I say. "Do you hate it?"

Her lips part, but all that comes out is the sound of troubled breaths.

So I slide down underneath her shirt again, creeping up her skin until I reach the roundness of her breasts.

Her breathing picks up. "It makes me feel…"

"Scared?"

She shakes her head.

"Excited?"

The blush on her cheeks only gets redder.

She doesn't have to say her thoughts out loud for me to know what she's thinking. I can feel it from the way her body responds to my touch. She craves me. She just doesn't know what to do with that bottled-up feeling. She fears the unknown.

But I can give her something she'll recognize.

My hand briefly skims her nipples, and when she sucks in a breath, I pinch it and lean in to press a kiss right below her ear.

She gasps, and it almost turns into a moan right there and then.

So sensitive. Almost like she's never been touched at all, not anywhere. And it makes me wonder just how sensitive.

I continue toying with her nipple, flicking and tugging it while pressing delicate kisses on and around her neck. Her head tilts backward, and a soft moan escapes her lips, making my cock bob up and down again.

I love the way she sounds and how she writhes against the palm of my hand as I play with her nipple. And when I bring my hand to her other breast, she begins to rub her legs together.

A filthy smirk forms on my lips as I relentlessly play with her, alternating soft kisses with painful tugs until her entire body starts to shake and heat.

"Oh God," she murmurs. "This feels so …"

"Good?" I fill in.

She simply nods, breathing ragged breaths as I play with her tits underneath the flimsy fabric of the shirt she's wearing. My shirt. On *my* girl.

Because she is mine, whether she wants to be or not.

My owner gave her to me, and she is mine to play with as much as I want. And now that she's finally letting me get close, I'm not going to let this opportunity slide.

I alternate the tugs between her two breasts, pressing wet, succulent kisses near her collarbone and under her ear. I roll her nipple between my fingers and listen to the sound of her breaths, the movements in her chest, the scrunching of her fingers around the fabric of her shirt, and I realize she's close.

I whisper into her ear, "Show me what it looks like when you fall apart."

Right then, I tug and twist so harshly that she moans out loud, and her body begins to convulse. I hold her steady with one arm while the other continues to play with her nipples, her muscles tensing against mine in sweet bliss.

By the time I'm done, she's huffing and puffing, and I lean back and look into her eyes.

"I don't understand. What just happened?" she murmurs.

"You came," I muse, biting my lip.

Her face turns bright red. "I didn't even know that was possible."

I can't stop the smirk from forming on my face. "You're more sensitive than any other girl I've touched."

"What?" she mutters.

My hand slips down her chest, and I immediately curl

down her panties.

"What are you doing?" She's still heady from her orgasm, but I know she knows what I plan to do.

"Did you think I was finished?" I groan, and I dive into her panties. "Let me feel how wet that made you."

The second my hand cups her pussy, her body freezes but then relaxes when my middle finger rests on her clit. I slowly but steadily circle her clit, then slip down her slit to coat my finger with her ample wetness.

I slide back to rub it all over her sensitive little clit, which still thrums with desire. I know she won't push me away, not when she's this needy.

So I circle her clit while gazing into her eyes, dying to see that same sweet explosion again. Because that look on her face when she falls apart is everything to me.

Everything about her fascinates me to the point of obsession, and I want her to know.

I want her to know how badly I crave every inch of her skin.

Every breath, every lick, every moan.

I want to consume her very soul.

I want it all and so much more.

But this … this is a good start.

My cock hardens again from her ragged breaths and wetness spreading all over. My finger on her clit flicks back and forth quicker and quicker until her breathing rises and her fingers scratch the walls, desperate for something to hold on to.

"That's it, beauty, come all over my fingers."

She moans out loud, and wetness spills from her pussy, covering my hand entirely as I flick her thumping clit. When her breathing finally stops coming in waves, I stop, but my hand is still there, cupping her pussy. The same pussy I can't wait to bury my already hard cock in.

"Fuck," I groan, and I press my lips to hers, claiming her mouth too.

These lips of hers were made for kissing. The way she yields when I lick the roof of her mouth is nothing short of pure ecstasy to me.

The more I take from her, the more I need. It'll never be enough.

Not even freedom could weigh up to this.

My lips separate from hers, and I blink a couple of times, staring into her eyes.

Freedom.

Or this girl.

Never once did the thought ever cross my mind.

Until now.

She stares back at me, lips swollen, cheeks flushed, her body still hot from my fingers splayed across her pussy.

And I realize then and there that I crossed a line I wasn't supposed to cross.

Because there is nothing I live for … except freedom.

But now there is her.

***

AURORA

Suddenly, Beast pulls away, and I'm left completely confused by what just happened.

One moment, his hands were under my shirt and in my panties, and then the next, they were gone as if they were never there to begin with. As if I didn't just have the most amazing orgasm. And not just one, but two right after each other.

All because of him and those amazingly skilled hands of his.

The same hands that kill people every day.

I shudder against the wall and push the lust out of my head, forcing myself to come back into the here and now. But damn, is it hard to look away as he drags his pants back up his muscular ass.

I swallow away the lump in my throat and try to cool myself off by opening the faucet and sticking my hands underneath. The cold water feels nice, especially when I splash some of it on my face and drink some.

But the cold can't erase the heat in my body or the warm glow in my heart.

You did it. You actually did it, Aurora.

When I lift my head again, he's sitting in a corner far away from me, the look on his face grumpy. As though I did something wrong.

But I didn't do anything except completely lose myself in the moment, just like him. I know he liked it when I licked him, and I definitely know he liked feeling me up, making me all hot and bothered. The sounds he made were proof.

But then why can't I shake this feeling that he's angry?

Suddenly, the door at the top of the stairs opens up again, and Raymond slowly comes down the stairs. There's a container in his hands, and it draws all the attention away from his gloomy face. I find myself hovering toward the bars, and when he opens the lid, my mouth begins to water.

Bread.

And meat.

But the bread smells so nice my stomach immediately begins to growl.

"Don't know what you did to please him, but …" Raymond mutters, chucking the bread through the bars. "Here you go."

I manage to catch it and chomp down on it before he has a chance to steal it away from me.

The meat is slung in as well and lands right in front of Beast, but he makes no effort to reach for it whatsoever.

"Beast. Dinnertime," Raymond says, laughing. "You're gonna need it for tomorrow."

"Tomorrow?" My eyes light up. "What's tomorrow?"

A smirk grows on Raymond's face. "Yeah, I bet you'd like to know, wouldn't you?"

This bread suddenly tastes a lot more sour.

"Too bad we don't explain our business to a goddamn prisoner," Raymond spits. "Now be a good fucking girl, shut up, and do what you're told while you're here."

"Don't talk to her like that."

Beast's voice alone already brings goose bumps to my skin.

I can almost feel his eyes burn into my back.

"Fuck you," Raymond growls at him. "You should be glad I'm still feeding you after what you did."

He slams the bars, making me jolt back with the bread still in my mouth.

"I'll see you at dawn," he adds with a sneer, then he marches back upstairs, slamming the door shut.

I munch down on the bread, and my stomach finally doesn't feel like a gaping hole anymore. But the Beast is still sitting in his corner, gazing at the piece of meat like it's his nemesis.

"What's wrong?" I ask.

He simply frowns, and it makes me feel like it's me that's the problem.

I pause, biting down on the bread. "Did I do something?"

His eyes flick to me, and it takes him a while to respond. "No. But I did."

Now I'm even more confused.

I sit down on the ground too, and look at him the same way he's looked at me.

Is this about what Raymond said? "What happens

tomorrow?"

Beast merely shakes his head, and my stomach drops. Even though the food in my hands smells appetizing, it's suddenly become hard to even look at.

"Are you hunting my papa again?" I ask.

"Don't ask questions you don't want answers to," he replies with a grumpy tone.

I suddenly feel cold. Like this cell isn't big enough for the two of us.

"What if you just decide to run instead?" My voice is a lot louder than normal, but I can't stop the emotions from flowing out.

The room fills with a kind of heaviness I find hard to describe. Intangible, but present nonetheless.

He points at his neck. "The collar. It activates instantly when I go out of a certain range."

I lower my eyes and sigh.

"What?"

"I just don't want you to kill my father."

His eyes narrow, and he finally reaches for the meat and takes a giant bite. "I don't either, but I do what must be done."

"What must be done?" I parrot, incensed he'd talk about it so easily as if his life means nothing.

"I didn't choose this," he says.

"I didn't either, yet here we are," I reply, also taking a big bite, despite the fact that I'm nauseous from the clear admittance he's going to try to kill my father again.

I know I promised Lex I would help him find my father, but I only said that to get him to stop. I don't actually want my father to get hurt or die. But Beast … he'll surely kill my father without question because that's his job.

But I don't want the conversation to die out either now that I've finally gotten him to talk instead of grunt.

"How did you ever end up in this cell?"

His brow rises. "Does it matter?"

He sounds annoyed. Still, I feel like if I'm going to try to persuade him to help me get out of here, I need to know more about him. I need to know if I can trust him.

"I just feel like …" I tuck a strand of hair behind my ear. "If you kiss people, you should get to know them."

He swallows a piece of meat and pauses. Seconds feel like hours as his lips part. "I was young. In the streets. Then I was snatched."

"Snatched?" My eyes widen. "As in … taken? Off the streets?"

He nods as if it's the most normal thing in the world. "I was sold. Trained. Hurt." He shows me the scars on the back of his arm and points at his face. "Taught how to kill."

"Like an assassin," I say.

He grimaces. "Like a hound."

Eighteen

BEAST

Past, age 8

I run across the street and bury my nose into a trashcan, trying to find the leftovers a couple just threw inside. A half-eaten burger and some fries make my stomach roar. I fish them out and rush off to the side of the building, where I sit down behind a dumpster and munch down on the food before it's no longer good.

It's been a while since I had a decent meal, but this comes close.

A rat rummages around in the garbage in front of me, and he knocks over some smelly trash. Its little nose wiggles, and it comes crawling my way, eyes aimed at my delicious burger.

My stomach growls, and I look at the burger in my hand and then the little rat staring at me.

Sighing, I pluck off a piece of the bread and hold it out to him.

It grabs the piece with its little paws and quickly scurries off to eat it somewhere else.

A smile grows on my face.

Even though I'm hungry, I know others are too, and I'm never too hungry not to share.

I take another bite of the burger, savoring the taste until it's all gone.

I'll have to go out there soon to try to find something to drink as well.

I tilt my head and peer behind the dumpster at the people walking down the street, oblivious to their surroundings. No one ever notices me here. Only when I come out to take something I don't own do they see me. When I intrude into their space like an unwanted visitor. A nuisance.

It's the reason I usually stay hidden and sleep until the moon appears.

During the night, I come alive.

And I'm definitely not the only one.

But I rarely make contact with other homeless. Nothing beyond a simple glare.

I've learned not to trust anyone or anything. The things

I have get stolen often, so I've grown wary of anyone coming close.

I stare up at the darkening sky, watching the stars appear one by one. It's almost time.

Suddenly, a van stops in front of my little alleyway, and I stop moving entirely. Two weird-looking guys step out, wearing thick trench coats, faces hidden behind thick scarves. I stay hidden behind the dumpster, only leaning sideways to take a peek at what they're doing, hoping they'll be gone quickly.

Suddenly, one of them looks directly at me.

I instantly push myself back and close my eyes for a second.

Until I hear the footsteps.

"Hello, little kid."

Chills run up and down my spine.

"What are you doing out here all alone?"

I don't answer. I have no clue what to do. I want to run, but they've blocked my only exit.

"I just wanna talk, that's it. Where are your parents? Are they around here somewhere?" he asks coyly.

I don't trust these men one bit. What if they're here to mug me?

"Why are you hiding? I'm not going to do anything Where's your family? Do you even have any?"

Fuck. They're looking for my weaknesses.

I search around in my plastic bag for anything I can find. I've got some cans that I was going to recycle for money, and I know those lids are sharp. But damn, I wish I had a knife right now. I should've stolen one when I had the chance the other day.

"Come out, little boy. I know you're behind that dumpster," the man says.

I swallow, but my throat feels dry.

Without thinking, I tear the lids off the cans and stuff them in my pocket, then chuck the cans at the guy.

"Hey! Stop it!" the man yells. "Need a little backup, this one's feisty!"

I keep throwing them, but they're getting closer and closer, and all I can do is walk backward farther into the alley until my back hits a wall.

Two of them come storming at me, and I've got only one option left. I fish the can lids from my pocket and swing them wildly, cutting into their skin as they grab me.

"Put me down!" I scream.

"Jesus Christ," the man barks as he swings me over his shoulder. "Calm the fuck down, kid."

"No! Let go of me!" I fight as best I can, punching and kicking all around.

The other one ties down my feet while I try to kick him away, but it's no use. I'm only a kid, and they're much stronger grown-ups. "What a monster. This one will fetch a big price, I'm sure."

A big price? What the fuck?

"What are you doing?!" I shriek as they carry me out of the alley.

The man following the guy who's picked me up looks up at me with a devilish gaze. "You're coming with us, kid."

My pupils dilate. Oh no. I've heard about this from other kids, but I never believed the stories were true.

Until today.

I'm flopped down onto a hard surface, knocking the air from my lungs. All around me is metal and black leather. The van.

"No, no, no," I mutter as I crawl up to my knees.

The guy quickly shuts the door before I can even try to get out.

I bang on the door and the windows. "Let me out!"

They open the front doors and step inside while the van wobbles sideways from their weight.

"Where are you taking me?!" I yell into the thick metal bars separating us.

The guy in the passenger's seat turns his head, the smile on his face as rotten as the words he speaks. "The Netherlands."

"What?" I gasp.

"Our clients will love a little fighter like you," he muses morbidly. "After you've been trained to behave, of course."

I shriek and punch the bars, but to no avail.

"Scream as loud as you want. No one's going to hear you now, kid." He grins. "There's only one thing street rats like you are good for … to be sold to a wealthy Dutch mobster."

***

Aurora

I gulp. No wonder he doesn't even behave like a normal human. He's been stuck in cages all his life. He said he'd been here for years, but I never understood just how long that meant. How deep this depravity goes.

All this time, he's been hungry. Hungry for food. Hungry for the outside world. Kept on a leash and forced to do the bidding of whoever owns him.

My face softens, and I can't even look at the bread without tearing up.

"Why are you crying?" he asks.

"Because …" I don't know what to say.

I thought I knew what hardship was. The things I've witnessed, the things my papa did to other people, killing them in cold blood, that was harsh. But this? This is on another level.

"I don't want your pity," he growls.

I brush the tears away. "I'm not pitying you. I just find it hard to digest."

"It's my truth. My world," he says with a growl, and he takes another big chomp out of the meat.

His world.

This world of fighters, survivors, and boys who live on the street.

This world I only saw a tiny glimpse of when my papa took me with him on his business trips.

"What about your parents?" I ask.

"I don't have them," he says.

I blink a couple of times. "Like, never?"

"They died."

He says it so matter-of-factly that I wonder if he feels nothing or feels too much.

"I … I'm sorry."

"It was years ago," he says, gazing at me in a stern manner. "It doesn't matter."

"Well, I think it does," I say, taking a small nibble of my bread. "Everyone needs parents. I couldn't bear to lose my papa." It's out before I realize it, and it makes it hard to swallow.

"You will," he states. "Everyone dies."

"I know …"

I hate the thought. I don't want the people I love to die. I don't have that many people to love. But he states it so matter-of-factly, like he doesn't even care, that I'm starting to wonder if it's indeed a weakness of mine.

"What about your mother?" he suddenly asks.

"W-What?" I mutter, caught by surprise.

"Your mother, you never spoke of her."

"Oh." I avert my eyes. "She … died."

"I'm sorry," he says.

"It's okay. I mean, I guess you can't miss people you never knew," I reply, and I look up at him again. "But I do wish I could've gotten to know her. Even if only for a day. My father always said she was beautiful, with flowing black hair and pearly white skin like Snow White. He hated that I looked like her."

"I don't," he says. "I don't hate you."

I can't help the tiny smile from creeping onto my face.

"So how did you grow up?" he asks.

I don't really know how to answer that without sounding incredibly insensitive.

"Oh, you know … with my papa. You've seen the house. He took care of me," I say, rolling my eyes out of embarrassment.

"What's he like?"

I avert my eyes. "Strict. But he's only like that because he loves me."

"Because of *love*?" he growls.

"Yeah," I say, taking a bite of my bread. "He wants to keep me safe. That's why there were so many rules."

"Because he's a mobster," he fills in, finishing his meat.

"Yes, but that's not all. I mean, it's tough being his daughter. But I'm really grateful for all the things he's given me. I'm thankful I've been able to live a life of luxury. And I don't mind the strictness. I don't want to be a burden, you know?"

"A burden?" He frowns.

"Ah, never mind," I say, wishing I never said it out loud. "I don't want to sound like I'm complaining. You know, compared to what you went through."

"Why would you be a burden?"

His question catches me off guard, and all I can do is stare with my lips parted.

"You're beautiful. Smart. Resourceful," he says.

The bread drops from my hand.

What?

Did I just hear that right?

My eyes widen, and my jaw drops even farther. Slowly, my entire face heats.

No one has ever said those things to me.

"Don't believe me?" he asks like it's a test.

I shake my head. "No, how do you—?"

"I've seen enough to know it's true."

I'm too shocked to even know what to say. "How?"

"You cried when you had to give up your papa to save yourself. You still defend him. You tried to defend me."

Good God, I didn't think I could blush any harder, but apparently, I can.

"I don't know your name, but I know you have a good soul."

Tears well up in my eyes. "My name is Aurora." I can't hold them back. "But I am not beautiful."

Nineteen

Aurora

Past, age 10

"Hey, Aurora," my bully echoes through the hallways. "Oink oink, pig!"

I'm mortified. People all around me laugh. There is nowhere to run, nowhere to hide. Even though not all of them know me, I still feel watched. Like they know he's talking about me.

And it makes me do a u-turn into the girl's bathroom and slam the door to my stall shut.

I sit down on the toilet and bury my face into my gloved hands, rubbing at the tears which refuse to stop

Why can't I stop? I don't want to cry, not because of him.

I wish things could've been different. That I'd listened to my father's warnings about kids my age. That I'd trusted him when he told me they wouldn't accept me.

My hand dives into my pocket, and I fish out my phone, vigorously typing in the chat to let it all out.

Me: It happened again. Timmy called me a pig. I can't deal with this. I'm in the bathroom. What do I do?

It takes my father a while to respond, but when he does, my head hangs, and I breathe a sigh of relief.

Papa: That's it. I'm taking you out of this fucking English school. Fuck the laws here in the Netherlands. You're old enough anyway. I'll have my driver pick you up in ten.

Wait, what?
The laws?
What do the laws have anything to do with—oh.
It slowly begins to dawn on me.

Father didn't just send me to this school because I begged him to. He probably didn't even have a choice and had to send me here, regardless of whether he wanted to.

No wonder he kept me at home for as long as he could.

Tears roll down my cheeks and stain my gloves. My beautiful, beautiful gloves.

If only I hadn't taken them off, even if it was only for a second so I could wash my hands in the girl's bathroom. Maybe then I could've stayed here and pretended, if only just for a little longer, that everything in my life was picture perfect.

**

BEAST

Present

Tears have never persuaded me to feel anything.

Except with this girl.

"Aurora," I repeat, my voice dark, heavy, obsessive.

The word rests on my tongue like a piece of candy I can't wait to suck.

A beautiful name for a beautiful girl.

Yet she doesn't see it like that.

I scoot closer to her, closing the gap between us. Even though I was mad at myself for kissing her and wanting her more than anything I've ever wanted before, more than freedom itself.

But I can't stop myself from inching closer and closer, and I grab her face and press my lips onto hers before she can stop me. Before I stop myself.

Her lips are tantalizing, hot, and everything I could ever dream of.

But that's not why I want to kiss her.

Why I want to steal her tears and kiss them away.

"Stop," she mutters, and even though she says the words, her lips still move with mine.

"Then show me why," I say as her tongue twirls around mine. "Because you are beautiful in my eyes."

When she pulls away, all I want to do is hold her tight.

I don't know why. I don't recognize these feelings.

It's too hard to look away from her tearful face, and I want nothing more than to take those feelings away.

What does it mean?

All my life, I believed I favored nothing but freedom until she stumbled into my life.

She gets up from the ground but struggles to stay put, her legs quaking. She almost falls back against the bars, and I instantly jump to my feet.

"Are you okay?"

"Yeah, I'm fine," she replies, shaking her head, but I can tell she's not. Her eyes have been unfocused, and she's clearly straining to stay awake.

"You need sleep," I say.

"What?" She looks up at me, "No, I'm fine."

But after that sentence, she immediately yawns.

I move to my stash of straw and pile it up into a neat pillow. Then I march to her and grab her hand, forcing her to come with me as I direct her to the makeshift bed. With my hands on her shoulder, I push her down slowly until her legs crumple. She finally caves to the pressure and lies down.

"I don't understand," she murmurs as her head rests on the straw.

"What?"

A slight smile follows, and it warms my soul.

The soul I thought I'd long forsaken.

"This is your bed," she says.

"I can share," I reply.

She bites her lip, tears welling up in her eyes again, and now I'm the one who doesn't understand. "Why are you sad?"

"I'm not," she says, and she laughs a little.

Now I'm really confused.

Who cries and then laughs like it's funny to be sad? Only this strange girl.

"I just wonder why you're suddenly so nice to me," she says.

"Is that why you're crying?" I ask.

She nods, tucking her hands underneath her head. "I just never expected such kindness."

"From a beast?" I fill in.

She doesn't say another word, but the blush on her face tells me enough.

"I know what I am," I say, a kind of darkness overwhelming the warmth that had just warmed my soul. "But it doesn't make me a villain."

"You're their hound," she says, her voice filled with

dismay.

"Exactly."

I lean in and whisper into her ear, "Sleep. I will watch over you."

The second I move away, her eyes have already closed, and she looks like a sleeping beauty, waiting to be kissed.

But I'll restrain myself, just like I've always done.

Not just so she can sleep … But because I always have to remind myself of the consequences of kissing a precious thing like her.

The unraveling of my heart.

***

Aurora

When I wake up, I blink a couple of times, wondering how I fell asleep so quickly. Was it all a dream, or did I really just sleep for hours on end?

Good God, I needed that.

I yawn and look around, but I don't see Beast anywhere, and my heart begins to flutter. He was so sweet when he told me he'd watch over me, and I was too tired to reject his offer.

But now that I've finally slept, I need to come to my senses fast.

I sit up straight and look around until I find him huddled in the corner of the cell, gazing at the wall. I watch him for a few seconds, but he doesn't move.

What is he doing?

"What are you looking at?" I ask.

He glances at me over his shoulder. "Oh, you're awake."

I hear something scratchy coming from behind him, and then he turns to face me. "Just a bug. I tried to grab it, but it ran off."

I smile at him, but I don't really know what to do with it. Why he would want to grab a bug is anyone's guess. But I don't want to judge too quickly. These walls could make anyone insane in a matter of days.

"How do you feel?" he asks.

I smile. "Better."

Suddenly, the door above the staircase opens and in pours more light. I block my eyes because it's too bright.

"Rise and shine," Raymond says as he stomps down the stairs.

Beast and I both move away from the bars as the man comes into view, twirling the keys in his hand.

"Guess what you're gonna do today?" he says with a filthy grin.

"If it were up to me, I'd know exactly what we would do," I snarl back.

The dude stops smiling entirely. "And what's that? Smother me with a piece of bread?" He snorts again.

"No," I say. "I would steal those keys and—"

"Shove them into your eyeball," Beast interjects.

Raymond is taken aback by his comment and leans away, clutching the keys tight. "In your fucking dreams, Beast."

Two more guards walk down the steps, one carrying a peculiar-looking metal device.

My pupils dilate.

The collar.

Beast's body grows rigid at the sight, and he braces himself against the wall.

"Time for some fun," Raymond muses, and he whips out his stun gun.

The door is opened, and he steps inside, along with his two buddies. "You wanna do this the easy way or the hard way, Beast?"

Beast's muscles pump up, and he steps in front of me. "I'll go." Then he glances over his shoulder. "As long as she is safe."

Raymond smirks, tilting his head. "You don't get to make demands." He hands the stun gun to the other guard and whips out his gun instead, pointing it at Beast's foot. "Our boss might need your strength, but he doesn't need your toes. Now choose."

The other guards approach him, one with the collar, the other with the stun gun, careful of every step they make.

I'm completely frozen behind Beast, terrified of what they might do. He grunts but doesn't move, his eyes on the guards like a wolf ready to bite their heads off. Every move they make is calculated until they get within a hair's breadth.

"Move away from the girl," one of them says through gritted teeth.

His lip twitches, and he doesn't reply.

ZAP!

The attack is almost instant, the stun gun striking him in the belly.

I shriek. "No, don't hurt him!"

Beast roars out loud while they haul him away from me and push the collar around his neck within a few seconds, locking it in place. He groans as he tries to straighten his back again, despite the pain in his abdomen.

Suddenly, the guards march toward me.

I push myself into the wall. "No, get away from me!"

The guards grab my arms, forcing them to my back until my wrists are locked.

"I told you not to touch her!" Beast growls, and he goes to lunge at them, but he collapses before he can even try.

He wriggles around on the floor, clutching his neck, scratching at his own skin. I can hear electricity sizzle. His neck slowly turns red.

Oh God.

"Stop it!" I yell at Raymond, who is pressing a button on a device. "Stop. Can't you see he's in pain?!"

"Exactly the fucking point," Raymond says, and the others laugh.

"There's no need to do this," I say as Beast struggles to even get up on his feet.

"No one gets away with trying to defy me," Raymond spits back, and he applies another jolt, causing Beast to buck and heave.

Without a second thought, I shove my full body weight into him, and he drops the device on the floor.

He immediately snatches it up before Beast or I can reach for it. Incensed, he turns to face me. My heart is racing, my breath quickening.

WHACK!

The slap is fast, and my cheek instantly burns with pain, but I refuse to show it.

"Don't you fucking try any of that shit ever again," Raymond growls at me. "You hear me?"

I don't respond.

Behind him, Beast rises from the ground, his frame blocking the only light in the room until he casts a shadow big enough to catch even the guard's attention as he slowly turns to look.

"You'll pay for that." Beast's voice is low and husky. Almost as if he's making a vow.

Raymond snorts. "As if you'll ever have a chance, wearing that fucking collar, dog."

Beast leans over, just a little bit, but it's enough to make the guard lean back.

"Not if," the Beast growls, his fist tightening. "When."

The way he says it is so threatening that Raymond gulps, his knees quaking. Just like mine.

"We don't have all day!" someone upstairs yells,

breaking the spell.

The guards immediately jump into action and drag me along toward the stairs.

"Wait, where are we going?" I ask as Beast and the other guards march up the stairs behind us like we're all headed to the gallows.

And the grin on Raymond's face is anything but comforting. "You'll see."

Twenty

BEAST

Normally, I'm the one driving this van.

The one in charge of the hit.

But now I'm out of control. Shackled. The one thing I despise.

I'm in the back of the van with her, bound to the van's interior. It's a deliberate choice by the guards. If I try to escape, I'll take the whole van with me, including her.

My fist tightens.

I've got to keep my cool.

Don't let them see what's underneath.

Be the hound. Be the killer.

Suddenly, a velvety soft hand snakes around mine, and I lose all sense of reality. All sense of who I am as I turn to look at the girl whose face has been covered by a bag so she doesn't know where we came from or where we're going. They made her get dressed in my owner's wife's clothes. A simple blue T-shirt and a pair of black leggings. It fits so snugly around her tiny frame that I wonder if she feels at all comfortable, despite being hooded.

Her gloved fingers slowly lace through mine, like a little lamb trying to huddle close, and I can't help but be moved by that simple gesture of trust.

Trust I haven't earned yet am given without a single afterthought.

My fingers close around hers, and the warmth her gloved hand exudes makes me gently squeeze. I've never cared about anything in my life, but for some reason, I feel the need to calm her down.

"Where are they taking us?" she whispers, her voice trembling as much as her body.

"Shhh," I whisper.

Talking will only make things worse.

And judging from the fact that my owner made me put on my protective gear, we're definitely going somewhere dangerous.

She swallows and leans back as the van drives on, her body swaying from left to right as the steering wheel is jerked. They're in a rush, it seems. The question is why.

The van comes to a full stop with screeching tires, and

within seconds, the doors are slammed open.

"Out," Raymond barks.

I step out and blink a couple of times to adjust to the sunlight. We're in front of a giant mansion with the doors left open and bloodied marks all over the ground.

The same mansion I stole her from.

Behind me, Aurora is lifted out of the van, the hood ripped off like she's going to get interrogated.

She hastily looks around the premises, her eyes widening as she soaks it all in.

"This is—"

"Your home." A car door slams shut, and my owner walks toward us wearing a gleeful smile. "Aren't you happy to be back?"

Aurora's face turns white as snow, and for a second there, I believe she might faint. "Why?"

My owner cocks his head. "You know why."

He flicks his fingers, and the guards immediately spring into action, grabbing Aurora and hauling her into the mansion.

I follow suit, not letting her out of my sight.

"You're keen to get to work," my owner muses as he glances at me over his shoulder.

I merely respond with a grunt because my eyes can't stop focusing on the guard's hands snaked around her wrists, his nails digging into her skin. Nails I'll be ripping out of his fingers once I'm free of this chain around my neck.

The house is filled with dirt, shards of glass, and blood.

Stained with violence. Violence I caused.

Aurora's body seems to grow more rigid with every step she takes inside, her footsteps softer, weaker, as though her knees are about to cave in on her. All of her pain mounting into one single glance across her shoulder, one single stare straight into my very fucking soul.

I swallow, but no matter how hard I try, the lump in my throat refuses to go down.

I walk toward the shot-through windows to keep an eye on what's happening down below, but my eyes can't help but zoom in on a broken piece of pottery on the floor right in front of it with crushed pink flowers all around it.

Aurora pauses in the middle of the living room. Right in front of the piano. The same piano I found her under.

Her whole body begins to quake, her eyes skidding back and forth across the bloodied floor, as though she's marking every spot where I shot down one of her father's guards. All the bodies have been cleaned, but the evidence still remains … inside her mind.

"That's far enough," my owner barks.

Everybody stops. All eyes are on Aurora, but hers only find mine in the dark.

The air is filled with electricity. Rage bubbles in each and every one of these men's hearts, waiting to burst out into the world like a volcano while they watch her gaze at the ruins of her past.

Her eyes finally find the piano, her fingers touching the keys without actually playing.

Suddenly, Raymond grasps her hand, whisking it up to inspect the glove. "You're gonna play with gloves on?" All the guards laugh.

She jerks her hand away. "Don't touch me."

"Or what?" he jests back. "You afraid someone's going to tear a hole in your dainty little gloves?"

"Stop," my owner interjects, and everything suddenly grows quiet. "I don't have time for this fucking nonsense." He beckons Raymond. "You, at the front door. The rest of you, stay on guard."

The guards immediately disperse, leaving just us three.

Along with a very tense atmosphere.

"What are we doing here?" Aurora asks, her lip quivering. "Or is this just so you can revel in the pain you've caused?"

My owner laughs. "Don't be ridiculous, girl." He gets close to her. Too close. "No …" When he grabs a strand of her hair and tucks it behind her ear, it takes every ounce of my self-control not to lash out and rip off his fingers one by one. "I want you to give me what you promised me. The account."

Her eyes widen, and she accidentally hits a false note on the piano with her thumb. "The account?"

"The money, girl," my owner hisses, his grip on her face tightening. "The PIN to the secret account."

"I-I don't know." She stumbles over her words, and judging from the panicked look on her face, this is not what she expected would happen. "I only know where he keeps his documents, not the actual—"

"I don't want to hear you stammering. Go find my fucking money," my owner growls.

This is going to escalate. I'm sure of it.

"They're in his office," she says.

"What are you waiting for?" my owner hisses at her, and he shoves her at the door. "Go."

She throws glances at me before walking into the office across the hallway, and I follow them, but my owner blocks the door with his hand firmly planted on the doorpost. "Not you."

My eyes narrow. "She can't be trusted."

Aurora's eyes flick to mine.

I know she heard.

I can feel it in the way she looks at me, her eyes filled with betrayal. But I have no other choice.

He cocks his head. "You think a meek girl like her could kill me?" He snorts. "You're just as ridiculous as she is."

"This place is a honeypot," I say.

He pauses right before he's about to close the door on me.

"Let me guard the office," I add.

After a while, he opens the door again and points at the window in the back of the office. "Fine. Sit."

In the corner. Like a dog.

My nostrils twitch, but I ignore the growing need to punch his face and move to the back of the room, exactly where he pointed, where I lean against the wall and keep a keen watch on him.

I don't know what she told him, but I do know one thing—her lie is about to end, and the fallout will not be as pretty as her. And there is no fucking way I want her alone in a room with him.

My eyes are on them both as she searches the room, opening all the drawers and sifting through the papers, her frown growing increasingly harsher. Sweat drops roll down her forehead as she paces around the room, back and forth, from one closet to another, desperately trying to find whatever it is she promised him.

"Well?" my owner growls, tapping his foot. "Where is it?"

"I know it must be somewhere in here," she says, and she grabs a stool and places it next to a bookshelf, hopping on top to reach for something above the shelves. She's not nearly tall enough to reach the box, but her fingers still manage to pry it loose.

"Hurry up!" he growls.

Just then, she loses her footing.

I sprint to her, catching her right before she falls.

The contents of the box spill out over the expensive flooring, but my eyes are transfixed on hers as they bore into mine, my hand firmly locked around her waist. Her cheeks grow redder with every passing second.

"What the fuck are you doing?" My owner's stern voice breaks our connection.

I clear my throat and release her from my grip as she

gets up.

"She fell."

"I have eyes, you dumb fucker," my owner barks. "Why the fuck do you even care?"

I stand, towering over him, and he steps back. Just an inch, but enough to tell me the truth.

If this collar wasn't around my neck, I'd gut him like a fish in a heartbeat.

He fishes the buzzer from his pocket, and I instantly take a step back.

"That's what I thought," he hisses. "Back in your corner, dog."

Aurora silently gathers the papers, tucking them into the box, but her eyes can't help but find mine every other second. I try to ignore it, for both her sake and mine.

"Is it in there or not?" he hisses at her.

"I-I don't know. I—"

He snatches the box from her hand and chucks everything onto the desk, shoving all the papers aside until he finds what he's looking for. I don't know what it says, but a bunch of numbers have caught his attention.

"Where's the PIN?" he says through gritted teeth.

"I don't know where it is," she replies.

Suddenly he grabs her by the collar and growls, "Tell me the PIN right now!"

With tears in her eyes, she shakes her head. "I told you, I don't have it. Papa never told me."

The way he's grabbed ahold of her makes my jaw lock,

and my muscles tighten.

"Don't lie. Tell me what it is, or I swear to fuck I will—"

BANG!

Guns.

All my senses immediately go on high alert.

Aurora's eyes widen as my owner releases her from his grip.

BANG!

The second shot shatters the window, and the bullet ricochets across the room.

My owner grabs the papers, but not in time before shots begin to fill the room.

And I know right then and there that this was exactly what I told him it would be.

"It's a fucking trap!"

***

Aurora

BANG!

The shots happen so quickly, they barely register.

"What the fuck…?!" Lex mutters as he crawls up and rushes over to us, shoving me aside so he can hide too.

It feels like my mind is going blank and my body grows numb as the bullets ricochet across the room. The sound is heavy and loud, yet the noise doesn't penetrate my ears.

All I hear is this ringing.

The god-awful sound of men crying, begging for their life as blood oozes from their veins.

And him.

There was him.

Oxygen is suddenly knocked from my lungs as I'm picked up and hoisted into a corner of the room. A desk is lifted and thrown in front of me.

I look up. Straight into his eyes.

The same man who once showered this house in blood.

Now towers over me, arms wide open, shielding me from incoming shrapnel.

And at this moment, all I can do is stare in awe at the sheer beauty of his power as bullets rain down on us. On him.

He roars out loud as the bullets continue to shower the room in smoke and fire. But his eyes remain on mine at all times, as though our connection is the only thing keeping him standing.

When the hail finally stops, his raging breath is the loudest sound in the room.

"Fuck," he grunts, blood oozing from his arm.

Panic sweeps over my heart as I look at all the dents in his armor. The floor around him is littered with bullets. He used his body as a human meat shield to protect us. To protect me.

It all happened so quickly it barely registered that he

grabbed me first.

Me, not Lex.

I swallow away the lump in my throat as I look up into his eyes, which flame with a kind of fire I've never seen before.

"We have to leave," he growls. "Now."

Lex immediately grabs his cell phone and calls someone. "Ambush! Ready the van. Call for backup!"

Suddenly, a loud bang at the front door makes me shriek.

"They're inside," Beast growls.

I gasp. "Who—"

My eyes widen as I realize the answer to my own question … and immediately forget everything that just transpired.

Of course. My father's men.
They've come to save me.

***

BEAST

Suddenly, Aurora jumps up from the floor, her eyes skittering away toward the door like a firefly that's found a light in the dark.

I brush off the dust and leftover shrapnel, ignoring the

pain as I go after her.

"Hey, where are you going?" my owner snipes, but I ignore him and run out into the hallway to follow her.

"Stop!" I bark, but she's oblivious to the world around her, including my voice.

She ignores me and runs straight toward the front door.

"Aurora, stop!" I yell, and I grab her by the arm before she goes too far.

"That's my father out there," she replies, her nails clawing at my fingers, trying to jerk free from my grip. "Let go of me! He's coming to rescue me!"

"He's not coming for you," I growl back.

She completely ignores me and slips out of my grip with ease.

"Beast, take me to safety," my owner barks as he steps out of the office with heavy breaths. "I need to secure these documents."

I'm torn between focusing on him, the man who owns me and controls this collar, and the girl who's captured my soul. Grunting, I flick my eyes between them on opposite sides of this hallway while everything slips out of control.

"My father's out there. He's waiting for me to—"

BANG!

The gunshot has her stopping halfway through the hallway.

In the doorway is a man with a semi-automatic. And it's pointed straight at her.

BANG!

Twenty-One

Aurora

The bullet grazes past my skin.

It all happens so fast it doesn't even register at first.

Until the blood appears on my shoulder, staining my shirt.

Shock makes my bones feel like solid wood lodged into the ground.

Why would they shoot me?

These are my father's men.

My lip quivers as I stare at the man in the front door, the man who just shot me, tears welling up in my eyes.

"Aurora!" As fast as a human possibly could, Beast

storms toward me, covering my body with his, wrapping me into a cocoon beneath him.

I shriek as more bullets cover the area in darkness. I'm terrified and nailed to the floor. Behind us, Lex cowers in a corner near the office door, clutching my father's papers.

When the hail finally ends, Beast turns his rage toward our attacker.

Everything happens so quickly. Within seconds, Beast has whipped out his knives and chucks them at the guy, who narrowly avoids them, only to shoot at him. His armor catches most of the bullets as he keeps marching at him. More guards appear in the doorway, some shooting at Lex's guards stationed outside the house. It's a chaotic scene with bullets and screams flying left and right with no end.

Beast runs like a bulldozer over to the nearest guy who tried to shoot me and grabs his gun the second he fires it again. The bullet lodges itself into the ceiling, and he snatches it from his hands and knocks him in the head with it. The guy collapses, but before his head hits the ground, Beast points the man's own gun at him and shoots.

BANG!

I close my eyes from the harshness, but when more shouts are audible all over the house, panic forces me to look. Beast spins on his heels and points the gun at the other end of the hallway, toward the office we just came out of, and shoots again.

BANG. BANG!

More bodies flop down through the window, and I

shriek when one of them flings a smoke bomb our way.

"Beast!" Lex yells.

But there's too much going on, so much even I can barely keep up, let alone Beast who is flinging his knives and shooting the gun left and right. Every throw is a hit, whether it's their heads, their arms, their calves, or even their eyes. It's as if he was trained to do this … Trained to murder as efficiently as possible.

Bodies drop to the floor like flies, just as I remember from the first day I met him. And the sheer amount of blood makes me huddle in a corner next to the staircase, hoping it'll end quickly. With my hands over my ears, the sounds aren't so loud anymore, but nothing can stop the quickening of my own heartbeat.

I don't wanna die, I don't wanna die!

"You …" A voice above me makes me tilt my head.

Someone's at the top of the stairs, peering down at me below.

A guard.

I recognize him as being one of my father's, and the mere sight of his face makes my heart jump.

Until a gun appears.

And it's pointed at both me and Lex.

"Watch out!" Beast yells as he shoots someone in the doorway, only to spin on his heels and fling a knife at the man at the top of the stairs. The knife lodges itself straight between his eyes, blood pouring from his wound.

I flinch as his body topples over the banister and flops

down onto the floor right in front of me, blood and guts splattering all over, including me.

Another guard stumbles in through the kitchen, but Beast shoots him down with ease.

As if all of this is normal.

Like second nature.

When there are no more gunshots, and all the dust and blood have finally settled, all that's left is a whole lot of corpses and tears.

Tears for all the lives lost today.

Tears for my father, who was not here to save me.

Tears for the men who pointed their guns at me.

What did I do to deserve their wrath?

Beast approaches us and shoots at someone already on the floor right beside Lex, who was still blowing out their last breath. Gone. All of them. Snuffed out like their lives meant nothing.

Lex pats himself down while gazing around and then focusing his gaze on Beast. "Are there still any out there?"

Beast shakes his head. "The guards have cleared the area. We have to leave now. Before more arrive."

Lex nods. "I'll get that fucker another time. At least I have a paper trail of the money now." Beast offers him a hand and helps him stand, despite the fact that his entire body armor is covered in dents from absorbing so many bullets. Some must've hurt him.

"Finally, you prove yourself useful," Lex mutters, taking in a big breath. "Let's go."

He walks past me like I don't even exist, heading straight outside into the safety of his men's watchful gaze while I sit here in a corner of the hallway, gazing at the shambles of what was once my home.

Beast steps in front of my view, his feet alone so immense they block any sight of the body he just shot down from above. He goes down to one knee in front of me until our eyes are on the same level. And when his hand rises to touch my cheek, I flinch.

After all the blood and murder I just witnessed, something this soft and sweet feels odd. Out of this world. Just like him.

"It's okay," he says, blood trickling down his hand from the wound in his arm. "I won't let anyone hurt you."

Tears well up in my eyes. "But they were my father's guards," I mutter. "They shot me."

Without saying a word, he pulls me closer and pushes me into his chest, wrapping one of his big arms around my body tightly.

"You're safe," he says. "You're safe."

And for a moment, I stay there in his warm embrace, wondering what I've done to deserve all of this.

This hate.

This love.

This confusion.

And the mountain of affection growing deep inside me when I listen to this beast's heart beating ever so fast just because he's holding me. This heart filled with fury and death as he hugs with hands that have only known violence.

Over and over, he tells me I'm safe. But the more he does, the more I'm beginning to question whether he wants *me* to know … or himself.

Instinct makes my hands wrap around his body too, wanting to feel the crazy kind of devotion he showed by killing every last guard who even dared to point his gun at me.

One by one, all shot down until none were left.

And not a single time did he look at his owner to make sure he was okay.

The one man who holds his life in the palm of his hands.

It was this beast's job to save Lex.

Yet he saved me too.

Not because he was forced to, but because he chose to.

I swallow and lean away to look at his scarred, beautiful face, and for the first time since I met him, I don't see a monster … I see a man.

The man who wanted nothing more than to save this girl who ran so blindly into the arms of men who tried to kill her.

Blood oozes from the wound on his arm, and I realize a bullet must've hit him. My fingers instinctively hover close to it. His armor couldn't protect all the parts of his body, only the most important bits. But it must still hurt.

"Beast!" A guard's shrill voice interrupts us, and the connection is broken when Beast looks at the front door.

But his hand still slides down my arm and interlocks with my fingers as he pulls me along with him, out of this bloodstained house and away from the place I once called home. "Let's go."

***

BEAST

When we get back to my owner's house, I'm the one to immediately tear the hood off her face. I don't like it when they try to hide her from the world. Or when they try to hide the world from her.

I may not know much about this world, but I know beauty is hidden in its cruelty. And when I look into her eyes, I see a world of possibilities. A world I'd like nothing more than to dive right into.

But the fear in her eyes reminds me of my place in this world. Of hers as they herd her out of the van and back into his clutches.

"These papers cost me my men," Lex says as the door behind us closes, and we're in his office again.

"I didn't know they were going to be there," Aurora says, panic lacing her voice.

My owner sits down at his desk and places the paper

neatly in front of him, staring up at both of us like he's questioning our motives. "But you liked the surprise, didn't you?"

Her face contorts. "I don't know what you want me to say."

"Let's be clear. There is only one thing I want," he says. "Your father's head on a silver platter."

She swallows, her entire body beginning to shake. "I told you I would help you find him."

"Good," my owner answers. "Then our deal still stands."

I swallow. What deal? Is this the conversation she talked about earlier? The one where she said she had to give up her own father in order to save herself from him?

"Unless you'd like to go back on your end of the agreement," he muses.

"No," she quickly replies.

The mere thought of him putting his hands on her makes my blood boil, and I could punch a hole into the wall beside me.

"Good. You're lucky you found these papers for me," my owner says. "Or your fate may not have been so fortunate." He eyes me now. "You. You did well for once."

That doesn't sound at all like a compliment, but I'll swallow it down as long as it leads to something good.

"I thought bringing you would only do me more harm than good, but it seems like you managed to sniff out intruders before anyone else noticed," he says.

I didn't sniff out anyone, but I do know what a trap is, and that place certainly smelled like it.

"You kept me out of harm's way, and for that, you'll be rewarded," he says.

My ears perk up at the word reward.

"But first…" My owner snaps his fingers at one of his other guards. "Take her back to the cell."

"What? But I helped you," Aurora balks as the guard grabs her arm. "I did what you asked!"

"You didn't bring me a PIN or my money," my owner growls back. "You should count yourself lucky you're still alive, thanks to my dog."

Aurora grimaces as the guard drags her out the door, and I fight my body to stop myself from walking alongside her.

"Since you saved my life today, let me repay the favor, dog." He snaps his fingers at his other guard. "It's been a rough day. Have the maids prepare a bath in my guest chambers and see to it that the bed is made. And take care of his wounds, will you?"

A bed? A bath?

For me?

I'm dumbfounded by the sudden humane treatment, but when the door opens, and that same guard who hauled Aurora away comes back, a pang in my stomach prevents me from feeling anywhere near grateful.

"Sir," I intervene. "Thank you, but—"

"But what?" my owner barks. "You prefer something

else?"

"I want my cell." I tug at my collar. "And this collar off."

My owner looks at me like I've lost my mind. "You want to go back down there?" He laughs. "Well, I mean, I wasn't going to let you stay in my guest chambers for more than a day, but if you're so eager to go back down into that cage you call home, sure. Be my fucking guest." He snaps his fingers and points at my neck. "Fix him up and take the damn dog back to his pen."

He laughs again as the guard snarls at me the same way he always does when he's about to pull out his stun gun.

"I won't fight," I say as they take me out of the room and one of the medics checks my wounds.

I hiss when he shoves something inside a hole in my arm and takes out a bullet, showing it to me like it's some kind of prize I won.

"Just one this time, Beast. You're lucky," he muses, dropping it on a tray before sanitizing the skin around the wound and suturing it.

"Lucky …" I parrot, snorting.

"All done," the medic says, and he gives the okay to the guard, who brings me back to that door again.

The door that leads straight down into hell.

But down there, in that place I so despise, she resides.

Waiting.

Yearning.

And there isn't a fiber in my body that thinks about

leaving her there on her own.

So I walk down the steps with my head held high, waiting until she finally comes into view.

And when our eyes connect, I know for sure.

This girl …

I want her.

No matter the price.

Twenty-Two

Aurora

When the door to the cell opens again, I don't even care to look at the guard who shoves Beast inside. All I can focus on is him. The beastly man who saved me from death. Who protected me from my father's men when I believed they'd come to save me. Who towered over me to stop the bullets from sieving straight through me.

Not his owner ... me.

I hold my breath when his eyes land on mine, the air suddenly feeling too hot to breathe.

The door closes with a squeak, and the guard snorts. "And you choose this over a nice room? Enjoy your fucking cell, Beast."

When the guard has gone back upstairs again, my lips part. "A nice room? What did he mean?"

His armor is still covered with the blood of his enemies as he rips down the wires and unbuttons the pieces, dropping all of it to the floor until nothing is left but cargo pants and a thin black shirt.

"I was offered the guest room for the night," he replies, stalking toward me. "As a reward."

"And?" I ask, thinking you must be mad to decline something like that. A cozy bed, a warm bath, a semblance of humanity.

"I don't want it," he says in a single breath, his voice so low it causes goose bumps to erupt on my skin. "I want to be here."

Oh God. He truly has gone …

"With you."

Mad.

I shake my head as he gets closer and closer while I bump into the wall. "But why?"

He's right in front of me. "Isn't it obvious?" He grabs a strand of my hair and brings it to his nose, taking a deep, sensual whiff, causing his eyes to almost roll into the back of his head. The groan that follows makes it hard to breathe at all. "I want you and only you."

My pussy clenches simply from the sound of his voice.

I have to admit, the thought did cross my mind. Several times. But could I really give myself to this man? This beast?

He towers over me again, his chest pushing up against mine, and when his hand touches my cheek, my entire body zings with electricity.

God, why does my body respond the way it does to him? Why can't I resist the urge?

He leans in, lips dangerously close, eyes open, hungry, ready to devour. "There is no reward greater than for you to be mine."

His.

Oh God.

How badly my mouth wants to say yes.

And when his lips finally land on mine, my heart begins to sing.

How can something so wrong feel so right?

This beast of a man without a name, kissing me like I am the only thing in this entire world that matters to him, makes it impossible to think about anything but him.

But I know deep down inside that it can't be true.

If we were outside this cell, in the real world, he wouldn't choose me. No one would.

But here in this cell, I'm the only thing he has. The only reminder of a life beyond these walls. And I realize I too am succumbing to brief moments of pleasure in the dark.

My head is spinning, going round and round as fast as his tongue swivels around mine. I'm helpless and lost in the onslaught of emotions, of wanting him as badly as he wants me.

And it scares me so much that I pull back for a moment

to gaze into his eyes, wondering if it's okay. If it's right.

But the way he looks at me makes me feel so out of this world that I can't help but blush.

"Is it so bad to be here with me?" he groans, pressing delectable kisses against the left side of my lip, drawing out a kiss. "Am I that terrifying? That gruesome?"

I shake my head slightly, not wanting our lips to detach even though I know in my head we shouldn't do this. But I can't help myself anymore, and neither can he.

After seeing what he'd do for me, how he protected me with his own body, I want nothing more than to worship his.

"No, on the contrary. I just wanted to say thank you," I mutter between kisses. "For saving me."

My hand slides around his neck, and I pull him closer, kissing him back with as much fervor as he kisses me. My other hand slides down his firm chest, along every ridge of his muscles, until I find the edge of his shirt and snake underneath.

I can't stop myself anymore. I need to feel his skin against mine. I need him to feel alive. To breathe. Because with every kiss, he steals more and more of mine.

It's as if he can read my mind because he suddenly, and very roughly, tears off his shirt and chucks it in a corner, his muscles flexing with every move. And my eyes can't stop taking it all in, almost tempted to lean in and take a lick.

God, what has happened to me?

In this cell, I turn into something else. A different kind

of monster. A monster of his making.

I gulp as he steps forward and grabs my hands, trying to push down the fabric of my gloves. I pull away and shake my head, then guide his hand down to the rim of my shirt. He hooks his fingers underneath, pulling it over my head. My breasts bounce in his face, but all he can focus on are my eyes. But his hands find their way up, trailing along my skin ever so softly, like he's memorizing the feel of my body against his fingertips until he reaches the peak of my nipples. I suck in a breath when he toys with them, finding it harder and harder to resist.

"I want to lick you, suck you," he murmurs, nipping at my lips. "Fuck you until you moan out loud for me."

God, I really shouldn't. Doing this would be for all the wrong reasons. But who am I kidding? I already lost the second his lips claimed mine, and now he's about to claim the rest of me, too. And I don't even mind.

As his lips press against mine, my hands slide down his body to his cargo pants, desire coaxing me to tug at the zipper until it comes loose. His lips momentarily tear away from mine as I hook my fingers around his underwear, his eyes boring into mine as though he's testing me and seeing how far I'll go.

But I've already taken this too far.

Too far to go back now.

I push the fabric down, down, down, until his cock finally springs loose, the size of him still managing to make my throat clamp up and my heart shoot through the roof.

You can do this, Aurora. And once you do, he won't ever betray you. You have Beast's trust. You have power.

"I want to take what's yours and make it mine," he growls. "I want to bury myself in your sweet, aching pussy."

Oh God. Why does it sound so … sexy?

One second, two exchanged looks filled with lust, and I'm done for.

His groans stoke the fire raging in my body as he lifts me from the floor with ease, shoving me up against the wall. My feet instinctively lock behind his back, his strong hands cupping my ass to keep me in the air. With a simple swipe, he tugs down my leggings, pushing my bare pussy against his body.

Oh, God, here we go.

I mewl with delight when he pushes the tip against my entrance, mere inches separating us, and he covers my mouth with his. Despite his crazy obsessiveness, I am completely smitten with this beast of a man. And I know in my heart this is my only chance. If I ever want to get out of here, I have to win this man over.

At least, that's what I tell myself is my reason for whispering, "Yes."

His fingers graze my clit as he pushes me down farther until there's no way back. And when he thrusts inside, my eyes almost roll into the back of my head. He's so huge and inside me, filling me up, almost as if he's completing me, and I've never felt anything quite like this before. I never thought losing my virginity would be this wonderful.

When he pulls back out, I feel empty until he thrusts right back in again, and my body feels whole again. And for a second, I wish I'd never have to come back down from this high because I've never felt more alive than I do now.

Is this what it's supposed to be like to feel loved?

To feel wanted?

It feels so wrong to enjoy it as much as I do. I was always told I would one day give this to the man I was supposed to marry, that it would hurt and that I'd hate it, but that it was my duty. But this ... I was never warned about *this*.

With every thrust, my mouth forms an o-shape until I can't help the little moans from escaping anymore. He sucks them all up one by one, kissing me between every thrust as if to silence me to stop anyone from hearing us so they won't try to stop us. Not that they even could.

Because I'm sure if they'd separate us, this man would tear them to pieces.

Beast is completely transfixed on me, his eyes brimming with lust so much it's as if he's been completely taken over. And I'm letting him take control.

In this cell, we have nothing but each other, and for some reason, I feel like it's all I'll ever need.

He groans louder and louder with each thrust, and I can feel his muscles tighten against me, his fingers digging into my ass as he holds me in place. My head tilts back as his lips roam freely across my neck, his tongue dipping out to lick every inch of my skin like he wants to savor every last drop of sweat rolling down my body.

I thought it would hurt, thought his cock would only give me pain, but the pleasure is overwhelming and not at all what I expected. I'm shocked by how badly I want this man, this beast of mine. And it scares me a little to know he wants me just as much. To know this man who could snap my neck with a simple flick would choose to bury himself inside me instead.

He groans and pulls back from the wall, only to carry me all the way back to his makeshift bed. He lays me down and crawls on top of me, all while his cock is still inside. His body is so huge it easily encompasses mine.

I gasp when he buries it to the hilt, my pussy thumping with greed. My hands drift from his neck to my face to try to hide because I'm so embarrassed. But he grabs my wrists and pins them to the floor, groaning against my lips.

"Don't try to hide from me," he says, hovering mere inches away from me. "I want to see you come."

My cheeks flush with heat as he pulls out and thrusts right back in again, gazing at me with what looks like pure wonder. And I'm helpless as he claims the last part of me that I kept to myself. Too late to stop the delicious orgasm from rippling through me as I fall apart underneath him.

He lifts me from the floor, still inside me, and kneels with me in his arms as he props me up on top of his legs. With one hand on my waist and the other around my neck, he begins shoving me down onto his length, burying his face between my breasts, kissing and licking my nipples. The size of him deep inside me almost makes my eyes roll into the back of my head.

"When you come, the scent on you riles me up and makes me want to… fuck."

He groans again and buries himself deep inside. So deep, I can feel his balls squeeze tight against my thighs. And I hold my breath when I feel something explode deep inside me, filling me to the brim.

My eyes widen.

Did he just … Come?

Inside me?

***

BEAST

Suddenly, she jumps off my thighs and falls to the floor, turning around to face me while my cock still spurts out its cum. My orgasm is still going, my cum flying all over as I grunt, seething with both rage and lust.

Why would she suddenly pull away?

"Oh God," she mutters, her fingers touching my slick strands of cum all over her belly instead of where it belongs; inside her.

My orgasm is ruined, but I won't let that stop me.

My fingers slide across her belly, through the cum, and I dip down to her pussy. Her eyes widen when I thrust not one but two fingers inside.

"Mine," I growl.

"Wait."

I grasp her ankles and pull her closer again. She attempts to crawl away, resisting me by clawing at the ground, and it confuses me greatly.

Why would she suddenly try to fight me after giving herself to me so easily mere seconds ago? One moment, she's begging me to claim her with my cock, then the next, she's panicking when I finally do give it to her.

I groan with frustration but still manage to drag her to me, holding her wrists so she won't slip away again.

"Beast," she murmurs as I pull her up to my thighs again with her back turned toward me and shove her back down on my dick, which is still hard as a rock.

She gasps with her mouth wide open as I thrust deep inside, so I grasp her neck and pull her head back so I can cover her mouth with mine and claim her moans too.

"Beast, I—"

Her words are interrupted by my thrusts, causing her to moan out loud.

"I want you on my cock now, woman," I groan

With her wrists pinned behind her back with one hand and the other on her waist, I shove her down onto my cock, listening to the sounds of her mewls as she comes undone. Her pussy is so tight around my dick and her body fits so neatly into me that it's as if we were made for each other.

And right now, I want nothing more than to feel her wet, aching pussy around my rock-hard dick as I thrust inside and spread my slick all over her. With her head tilted back, I finally have access to all the curves of her body and the delicious nipples that beg to be twisted.

"This body was made for me and me alone," I murmur into her ear.

My hand rises from her waist to her tit, and I squeeze tight as I bob her up and down on my thighs, twisting her nipple until she squeals. I love the sounds she makes, the way her pussy grows slicker the more I pound inside.

And when I grab a fistful of her hair and tilt her head back so I can kiss her neck, her arousing moans are what push me over the edge.

I roar out loud and thrust hard, burying myself to the hilt, jetting my seed deep inside her velvety pussy, not stopping until I'm finally satiated.

When I release her from my grasp, her body rolls off mine down to the floor, where she turns and stares at me, breathing out as loud as I am from the heavy sex. Her pussy is creamed, and when the cum begins to stream out of her, I push it right back inside.

I lean over her, our foreheads colliding, as I whisper, "My woman."

"Beast," she murmurs, the same way she did when she tried to crawl away from me, and I don't like the tone one bit.

My fingers pull out of her, and I lean back up again on my knees to gaze at her from a less arousing distance.

"Do you hate me so much?" I grunt, wondering if she despises herself for wanting me as badly as I wanted her. For giving herself to me.

Tears well up in her eyes. "No," she says, shaking her head.

I tilt my head and furrow my brow. "Then why did you try to stop me?"

Her fingers slip down her belly, through the slick, and touch the cum at her entrance. She gazes at it like it's foreign to her, like she could never imagine herself getting fucked the way she just did. "You came … inside me."

I lean over her again and press a kiss to her top lip. "I want my seed inside you." My hand hovers over her stomach, and I caress her belly where I was seconds ago.

She grimaces. "But that means … I might be pregnant now."

Her eyes suddenly roll into the back of her head, which drops to the floor.

Hard.

Twenty-Three

Aurora

Oh God, what have I done, what have I done?

The second I come to from my fainting spell, I blink a couple of times, mesmerized by the two emerald eyes staring straight into my soul.

Until I realize he's hovering over me with a concerned look on his face.

I immediately crawl away from him until I bump into a wall, yelping from the pain on the back of my head.

"Aurora." His voice is dark. Gruff. Chilling.

I'm heaving ragged breaths from the heavy sex we had, my mind still reeling with filthy thoughts from all the things he did to me. All the things I wanted him to do to me.

He crawls closer, dick still half-hard and dripping cum. I try to calm down, but it's impossible as I'm locked in this corner with that same cum dripping out of me.

Oh God, why did I do this? Why did I let him take me like that?

I thought it'd be easy to give him what he wanted, but I didn't realize he'd actually be able to … come inside me. Nor did I think of the possible outcomes.

He's so close now I can see the beads of sweat rolling down his skin. He leans in, his hand hovering close to my skin and caresses my cheek so gently I could die.

His jaw tightens, and he pauses midair, right next to my face. "Do *not* fear me."

My lip quivers.

"Not you too," he says, and I can't help but lean into the palm of his hand.

"I just …" I sigh out loud and close my eyes.

"What's wrong?"

"I want to slap myself for being so stupid."

He grabs my hand just before I do. "Don't."

"But I deserve it."

"No," he replies.

"Yes, I do," I quip. "I just had sex for the first time."

He cups my chin and says, "Open your eyes."

I can't help but obey. Something about his voice makes it incredibly hard not to.

"Did it hurt?"

I shake my head. "No, it felt amazing." My cheeks flush

again with heat just from thinking about it.

"Then don't feel guilty," he says.

He makes it all sound so easy when it really isn't.

"That's not why I feel stupid," I say.

"Nothing you do makes you stupid," he replies, still clutching my wrist as though he's afraid I might hurt myself if he doesn't.

"Yes, there is. What if I'm pregnant?"

He gazes at me like it doesn't even matter to him. Like the concept of being pregnant and having a child with him doesn't frighten him.

But it terrifies me to my core.

I can't have a … child.

In this cell.

"I don't want—" I can't even say the word out loud while he's practically hanging from my lips.

Suddenly, the door at the top of the stairs opens, and someone comes marching down so fast I can barely get my leggings up in time before they've seen me. It's Raymond, and he bursts out into laughter the second he spots Beast's dick.

"What the fuck have you two been up to?"

I throw my arm over my chest and make a beeline for my shirt, covering myself with it while Beast pulls up his cargo pants like it's no big deal.

"None of your business," Beast replies.

I can't even look at the guy. That's how embarrassed I am that he caught us naked.

Raymond marches to the door, whipping out his stun gun and threatening Beast with it. "You. Stay here. And you," he says, gesturing at me before pointing at the stairs. "Out."

Panicked, I scramble to my feet, staring at him for a second, wondering what the hell is going on.

"Are you deaf?" Raymond adds.

Beast snarls, but I quickly step forward before another fight breaks out. I don't want to see him writhing around in pain on the floor again.

"I'm coming," I say. "Please don't hurt anyone."

"Good girl," Raymond says, and he throws Beast a sneer. "At least someone knows how to listen."

Beast bares his teeth, but Raymond ignores him and grabs me by the arm, dragging me up the stairs.

My heart pounds in my throat. "Where are we going?"

He doesn't answer as he pushes me up and through the door. I blink a couple of times to adjust to the bright light.

Suddenly, Lex's face comes into view, and I almost shriek.

"Interesting," he muses. "I scare you, but that Beast down there doesn't."

I swallow down the lump in my throat. "How do you know?"

Lex snorts. "I know much more than you think." He circles me like a vulture, and it creeps me out. He turns around to Raymond and says, "Leave us." When he's gone, Lex focuses his attention back on me. "I'm curious to know why you choose to trust that monster."

"He's not a monster. He won't hurt me," I respond.

"Wrong," Lex replies.

My lungs feel like they're constricted. "You don't know him."

"And you do?" He stops in front of me. "Did you forget he already tried to kill you once?"

Sweat drops roll down my back, but I ignore them. "That was on your orders."

He steps closer, right up in my face. "And do you think I wouldn't order him to finish the job?" he says through gritted teeth.

Panic swirls through my veins, making my heart thump in my throat. "You need me."

"Do I?"

"I'm the only one who can get my father to talk."

"Yet his guards were so eager to gun you down too," he muses.

Tears well up in my eyes. "That was a mistake."

"Was it?"

I hate him. I hate his guts. "What do you want?"

"Oh, just a chat," he replies, groping his beard. "You see, there's something that's been bugging me for some time now — the fact that when we were at your house, bullets flying left and right, my hound first ran to you instead of me."

I turn to look at the stairs right behind me, sweat drops gathering at the small of my back.

"You wanna go back down there into that hellhole?" Suddenly, he slams me into the wall, right beside the door. "Be with *him*?"

"It doesn't surprise me he didn't go to you first," I quip.

But I regret it the moment I've said it.

"Exactly," he retorts, his jaw tightening. "And that's a problem. A problem that needs to be dealt with."

Why do I feel like this is a threat?

"You're cruel," I say, not knowing what else to say or do to make this nightmare end.

He laughs again. "Tell me something I don't know. In fact, tell me what the fucking PIN is so I don't have to lose more men to your stupid antics."

"I told you, I don't know," I hiss. "I've given you the papers. Isn't that enough?"

He slams the wall behind me, making me jolt up and down. "Don't play me for a fool!"

I slam my lips shut. Nothing I say is good enough for this man, and I have to be careful. He'd shoot me without a second thought if I got on his nerves.

"You're lying and stalling. I know exactly what you two have been up to down there," he says.

My eyes widen.

"Yeah," he mutters. "My guards can hear every breath, every sigh …" He leans in to my ear and whispers, "Every moan."

I shudder in place, feeling like my stomach is about to turn upside down.

All this time, I thought Beast and I were alone in that cell, but if the guards really can hear everything we do, everything we say, through that door …

Oh God, they could hear everything I told him.

"Do you enjoy letting him use you?" Lex asks.

Tears roll down my cheeks. "He wasn't—"

"You're a toy, Aurora!" he roars. "I gave you to him to play with." He shoves me into the wall and pinches my shirt until my throat is clamped shut. "Why do you like him? Tell me why?"

My jaw drops, but I don't know how to respond.

Have I gone insane down there?

Or does this man sound jealous?

"I don't know," I mutter.

"You don't know? Or you choose to look the other way, hmm?" Lex spits. "You know, I gave you the chance to stay in a comfortable room." His hand rises to meet my face, and he caresses my cheek with his gnarly claws, making me want to bite them off. "Yet you chose that cell instead. You chose to spread your legs to that goddamn beast," he growls. "Why?"

"Because I'm trying to get out!" It's out before I realize it. And I can't take it back.

Lex eyes me for a moment before finally releasing me from his grip. He shakes his head, and that same dirty smile appears on his face again. The one that makes me want to vomit. "You're using him."

I don't answer. I can't, and I don't want to.

But it hurts so badly to hear him say these words out loud.

He snorts. "You're smarter than I thought." He flicks his fingers again, and Raymond comes back into the hallway. "Bring her back down. I've heard enough."

When Raymond pushes me, I blurt out, "What, that's it?"

"I don't need information you don't have, little girl," Lex says, chuckling. "Have fun down there."

Raymond shoves me down the steps before I can say another word, but when I turn to look, Lex is still watching me with a raised eyebrow. And something about that doesn't feel quite right.

What is going on?

I walk down the steps as slowly as I possibly can, but Raymond pushes me so hard I almost lose my balance.

"Get back in your cell," he growls. "Now."

But all I can focus on is Beast. He's slouched in the corner, eyes turned away from mine, almost as if he's in pain. And I don't understand why.

Raymond pushes me inside and seals the cell door shut, then marches back upstairs. "Hope you enjoyed the show, Beast!" he yells before he slams the door shut so loudly my entire body jolts up and down.

But what truly makes my heart sink into my shoes is the way Beast turns to face me, his eyes hollow, completely void of any emotion.

Because as more tears well up in my eyes, I realize that

all of that conversation up there … was a trap.

"Beast," I mutter, "I—"

"Don't," he growls back, baring his teeth. "I heard *everything*."

Twenty-Four

Aurora

I can't stop the tears from rolling down my cheeks.

This is why Lex brought me up there.

Not to grill me about my knowledge of my father's affairs or his whereabouts. Not because he's jealous. But because I needed to break what fragile bond we were starting to have.

"I'm sorry," I mutter. "I—"

"Is it true?" he interjects. "Were you just using me to get out?"

I feel sick.

I didn't mean to yell that out loud. I didn't mean to say

what's been on my mind. And I didn't mean for any of this to go this far, but it did. And now I'm here in the cage, in the belly of the beast.

"What do you want me to say?" I respond.

"The truth, dammit," he says, and he slams his fists against the wall.

"I do want to get out," I say.

"By seducing me," he growls, glancing at me over his shoulder.

I shake my head. "It's not like that."

Suddenly, he storms at me and grabs my face. "Did you even like it when I kissed you? Touched your naked skin?" His fingers slide down my body, down to my navel, and I hold my breath. "Fucked your aching pussy?"

"Yes," I say, blinking away the tears.

"But it was all a lie." His voice is so dark I feel like he could cut through steel with a single roar.

Still, I shake my head. "You're wrong."

He lets go of me and marches back to his corner, the same corner I saw him sitting in when I woke up. There's a shuffling noise, but I can't tell what he's doing from here, and I'm too scared to get close. Even though I know, deep down, he could never hurt me.

Maybe that's why I fell.

"You used me." His words cut like a knife, hurting me more than his hands ever could.

Because the worst part is that there is some truth to it all.

"Did you think I would break you out of here?" he asks.

"No, it's not like that," I answer, swallowing the pain. "I just … needed a friend."

"A friend," he says, throwing me another hateful glance. "I don't have friends."

He turns around to face the wall again, and I can feel all hope draining from my body. Tears run freely down my cheeks as I sink to the floor and bury my face between my arms, locking them tightly around my knees.

I am not alone in this cell, yet I've never felt lonelier.

***

BEAST

I pull myself up and down from the rack hanging from the ceiling, but no amount of physical exercise can get rid of these demons floating through my head. I roar out loud and slap myself on the chest before I continue doing pull-ups. Anything to make these voices go away.

If only I hadn't fallen so deeply for a girl who wasn't mine.

I admit, she had me fooled.

Ever since she finally opened up to me and let me kiss her, I thought we had something between us. Something more than what could be contained by these bars.

But it turns out it was all a ruse.

A game she played just to break out of here.

And I fell for it. Hard.

I push up again and again while droplets of sweat roll down onto the ground, not giving a shit about how much my muscles are aching. I like the pain. It makes me forget.

Forget she even exists.

Because dammit, how much I need to forget about her right now just to be able to live.

Fuck.

I can't even look at her without feeling uncontrollable rage. Rage because she took something of mine that I wasn't willing to give.

My fucking heart.

On a platter.

Swallowed whole.

Fifty. Fifty-one. Fifty-two.

I count out loud in my head because it's the only way I can make the maelstrom stop. At least, it used to be before she came into my life. Before I let her take over my soul.

God, why can't I stop thinking about her?

Even when I know I should, I still can't get her teary-eyed face out of my mind, and it's humiliating.

She's only led me on and made me believe something that wasn't even there.

I should've used her as a toy, just like my owner wanted me to, and left it at that.

I blink, and in that one split second, I glance over at her

sitting in a corner, crying her eyes out. A pang of guilt shoots through my veins, and my elbow flops under the weight of my own body.

Fuck.

On the floor, I breathe in and out deeply, trying to get rid of whatever this feeling is that's nagging at me, but it refuses to go away.

"Why are you crying?"

She brushes the tears away. "Because … I'm sorry."

My nostrils flare. "You don't mean that."

"Yes, I do," she says.

"It doesn't mean anything coming from a liar," I say.

But that same pang hits me hard in the gut.

She weeps again. "Stop."

I frown. "Stop what?"

"You call me a liar, but I didn't lie."

"Yes, you did. You never told me you only wanted to fuck me to get out of here," I say.

"I didn't give you my first time just to get out of this cell!"

Her entire face suddenly turns red. Much redder than it ever was before.

Why do I have the feeling she did not mean to blurt that out?

"Never mind," she says, hiding her face again.

I shake my head. "I shouldn't have brought you here."

But I couldn't bring myself to kill her either.

I should've let her go.

I turn my head away, unable to look at the girl. If I'd done what I was supposed to, none of this would be so damn difficult. But even my own thoughts elude me sometimes.

"If you hadn't, I'd be dead," she suddenly says. "But in this cell, am I really better off?"

"Maybe," I reply, rubbing my sore arms from all the exercise.

"You made that choice, not me," she says.

"Would you have chosen differently?" I ask.

We look at each other, and for a moment, I feel that same serenity I always did when I looked at her ... before I realized how stupid I'd been.

"Does it matter?" she replies.

"Yes," I say. "To me, it does."

Her cheeks stain red again, and for some reason, a smile tips up her lips, something I didn't expect at all.

"Thank you," she says.

"For what?" I stop massaging my arms.

"For not killing me."

I frown and stare at her for a moment, the beauty in her eyes catching me off guard.

No one has ever thanked me, especially not for failing to do what I do best. And the sound of it is so unfamiliar, I don't know what to do with it.

"I was born to kill," I say. "But I didn't choose this life, just like you didn't choose to be here."

She nods. "But you don't want to be stuck in this cell

the rest of your life either."

I shake my head.

"Then you know why I told Lex that," she says. "And I'm sorry that I grasp at straws to get out of this cell. That I ever even thought of hoping you could trust me enough to help me escape," she says. "That I let you kiss me. Touch me." There's a pause. "That I gave you my first."

I swallow and take in the weight of her words.

Maybe she isn't just crying because she got caught.

"Why?"

"Because it hurts," she says. "It hurts to see you look at me like that."

I swallow down the rage I felt before.

It doesn't seem so important anymore.

"Do you feel something for me?" I ask, planting my hand against my own heart. "In there?"

She nods, and it sparks the fire I thought was doused.

"But I'm not perfect," she says.

"I'm not either," I reply.

"And I am not the only one who wants out of here," she adds.

Also true.

"Then you know what I'd be willing to sacrifice," she says.

I lower my eyes. "Trust. Dignity."

"My soul."

Her words are as heavy as my heart feels in my chest.

And it takes me a while to respond. "You and I, we're

not so different."

"Maybe not," she replies. "But you're a hypocrite if you think it's okay to murder people to be freed from this cell, but then judge me for using my body to get out."

"Hypocr…" I have trouble repeating the word she just used. I don't recognize it.

"My life, my family, are not your ticket out of this cell," she says.

Her words force me to look at her. "Just like I am not your ticket out of this cell either," I rebuke.

She looks down at the floor, drawing lines in the dust. "Then I guess we'll both rot in here."

Fuck. The mere thought makes my fingers coil up and my nails dig into my skin until it bleeds.

"Maybe I deserve to be in here," she mutters after a while, almost like she's talking to herself. She snorts. "Papa always liked seeing me in misery … now he's got his wish."

What?

Does she really mean that?

"Why do you care so much?"

She looks up. "What?"

"Why do you care about him if he makes you feel like that?"

Her pretty round lips part, but it takes her a while to respond. "He's the only family I have left. Of course I care."

"But does he even care about you?"

She gazes at me like she's seen a ghost, her face getting even paler than usual.

"You said your father would come and save you," I add. "But all his men have done is try to get you killed."

More tears well up in her eyes, and she turns around, away from me, but I can still hear her cry. I never expected it to hit me the way it does.

Maybe not everything is as a black and white as I thought it was.

And maybe I'm not the only one who's never felt love before.

I crawl toward her and wrap my arm around her. Even though I know she tried to use me… I've used her too. I used her tongue, her lips, her mouth, her skin, and made every inch of her body mine. So if she's the villain, then I'm an even worse one.

"I'm confused," she mutters. "I thought you hated me?"

"I do …" I say. "But I don't want to."

"I'm sorry," she says. "I don't want to use you to escape. I don't want to use anyone. I don't want to be the bad guy."

I haul her into my embrace. "No one does. But we all become one when faced with death."

She leans back. "Is that how you see it?"

I nod. "It's who I am because of this cell. A beast. A killer." My nostrils flare. "A monster."

"What if you could choose differently?"

Her eyes sparkle with a kind of hope that I've never seen before, and it moves me.

So much that I can't help but grab her face and smash my lips onto hers.

I know it's wrong, I know she doesn't want me, but I want her, need her, crave her soul to be mine.

And I kiss her as hard as I can before that sparkle in her eyes is lost forever. Because it's the only thing that keeps me from tearing a hole into my own body and ripping out my heart.

My hand snakes around her neck, pulling her in closer as I kiss her deeply, my tongue twisting around hers. Kissing her is like a dream I don't want to wake up from.

But the dream shatters the second I open my eyes and see these bars behind us, caging us in.

"God ... You are going to be the end of me," I murmur.

She gasps, her lips still red and swollen. "What do you mean?"

"I need to succeed," I say, licking my lips. "Or I will die in this place."

She swallows and pulls back, her face icy cold. "You mean you need to kill my papa."

"I have no choice," I reply, my jaw tightening, feeling the tension between us. "I must do what my owner wants from me."

"But he won't kill you," she says, and she pulls out of my grasp and stands up like she's suddenly turned to stone. "Why can't you fight them?"

I stare up at her from the ground. "Because that won't get me my freedom."

She glares at me without saying a word.

"Freedom," I reiterate. "*That* is the only thing that has always mattered. It's what he promised me."

She steps back, more tears welling up in her eyes. "But at what cost?" The look on her face hurts. "A heart." Her lips quiver. "Mine."

Her hand clutches close to her chest, and I realize this is why we were fighting. Why I thought I should hate her, even though I can't.

Because her heart is in this cage too, stuck between me and her father.

And it's going to tear us both asunder.

Twenty-Five

Aurora

I'm wildly awakened from a nap by Raymond rattling the cage with a baton.

"Get up," he growls.

I quickly crawl up from the floor, wiping the salt from my eyes.

I don't know how long I slept or how late it is, but I'm still tired. The days and nights are really starting to flow into each other down in this cell.

Raymond opens the door and, with a stun gun in his hands, throws a threatening look at Beast who's sitting in a corner. Then he chucks something inside the cell. Fabrics and shoes.

"Put that on," he tells me.

I slowly pick up the fabrics only to realize it's a giant purple dress, complete with slanted shoulders and ruffled edges near the bottom. Beautiful, if it was an ordinary dress. But nothing in this place is ordinary.

"Now," Raymond balks at me, as he closes the door again and walks to the front of the cage.

I don't think fighting them over this is worth it. "Can you turn around, please?" I ask.

Raymond raises a taunting brow. "No."

This is not going well. I swallow away the lump in my throat. "I can't do it when you're looking."

"Yes, you can," he says. "Take off your clothes." His voice is increasingly harsh and demanding as he steps closer to the cage, clutching the bars. "Or do you want me to do it for you?"

I cringe at the thought of having that foul man touch me again.

If my only choice is to undress while he watches, or have him put his hands on me, I guess the first is the least horrible option.

My fingers hook underneath my shirt, slowly pulling it up while I try hard not to burst out into tears for having to expose myself.

Beast suddenly steps forward, positioning himself between Raymond and me.

"Hey," Raymond growls. "Get out of the way."

"No," Beast replies, his arms folded.

I stare up at his back.

What is he doing? This is going to put him in danger.

"Walk away, Beast," Raymond says under his breath.

"You heard her," Beast replies.

My jaw drops.

Is he really trying to… protect me?

"You're blocking my view," Raymond growls at him.

"Exactly," Beast retorts. He glances at me over his shoulder. "Go ahead. I'll stop him from looking."

I'm too flabbergasted to even respond. But when he turns to face Raymond again, I quickly pull up my shirt. There's no time to wait. I have to do it now, while I still have privacy.

"You dumb fucking Beast." Raymond sticks his stun gun through the bars and shoves it into his belly. He groans with pain, but stays put, standing tall to block Raymond's view.

I pull off my leggings and take off my bra and panties, trying to be as quick as possible. But Raymond keeps shoving the stun gun inside, screaming, "Move!"

Beast won't budge one bit.

And it hurts so badly to watch him suffer like that as he takes strike after strike, the buzz crackling in the air like lightning, while I struggle to put on this dress.

"You motherfucker, when will you learn?!" Raymond shouts, pushing the stun gun into his skin so long Beast's teeth clamp shut, and I can hear him grunt in pain.

Tears sting my eyes, but I force them back as I pull up the zipper and put on the shoes. "Done," I quickly mutter. "Please, stop," I beg Raymond.

Beast goes to one knee as the current circulates through his body. When the stun gun is finally removed, he's breathing ragged breaths, completely spent.

"Don't fucking get in my way," Raymond growls. "Ever again."

Beast tilts his head to face Raymond. "Fuck. You."

The guard jabs him again.

"Stop!" I yell, rushing over to them. I shove the arm away so the stun gun disconnects. "Please, stop. I'm dressed. I've done what you asked."

"Your filthy cellmate needs to learn his place," Raymond spits back.

"And you need to learn to take a hint," Beast replies.

Raymond puts his fingers in his mouth and whistles loudly. The door at the top of the stairs opens, and more guards come down, one carrying that familiar collar, the one that makes Beast's eyes fill with rage.

"What's going on?" I ask as Raymond marches to the door and opens it up again under the threat of violence, wielding that stun gun like a sword.

"You're both coming upstairs. Now," he says, and he flicks his fingers at the other guards. "Strap him in."

It all happens so fast. One moment, I need to get dressed, then the next, five guards are fighting Beast for control. They push and shove, strike him with a stun gun and a baton, hurt him in every possible way, while all I can do is watch. I feel powerless as they bring him to his knees and force that same collar around his neck again, sealing him in his own death trap.

God, I hate what they do to him. How they degrade him to nothing more than a simple lap dog to do as they please. It's wrong on so many levels.

"I told you to fucking behave, Beast," Raymond says, and he spits on the floor. "Now do as you're fucking told, or we'll give you pain."

Beast rises to his feet, his head hanging, but his eyes blazing with a fury that I can only describe as terrifying.

"You're both coming upstairs," Raymond says, and two others whisk me away, up the steps.

I jerk free of their grip once there. "Stop manhandling me. I can walk."

Raymond grabs my arm and hauls me to the side. "You want a collar too?"

I shake my head.

"Then behave and do as you're told."

Before I have a chance to say anything back, they drag us through the hallway, into the foyer, and right into what looks like a dining room, complete with a giant table, where Lex is casually sipping a coffee.

"Ah, finally," he mutters, and he puts down his coffee and points at the chair. "Sit, sit."

The guard grabs a chair and signals for me to sit down. I don't think it's a good idea to rebel right now, so I do as he said.

However, the second Beast tries to grab a chair, Lex intervenes, "Not you."

The glare they exchange could light this whole room on fire.

"Stay at the door," Lex barks at him.

I glance at Beast whose only response is flaring nostrils as he puts his hands on his back and stands tall and proud.

Even now, when he's treated like vermin, he refuses to bow down, and I admire that.

I feel so out of place in this fancy purple dress, but the moment Lex claps his hands, I understand why he made me wear it. A whole bunch of waiters come in and place mountains of food on the table. Fresh strawberries, cured meats, all kinds of bread and buns, poached eggs, deliciously smelling bacon, and, to top it all off, a lavishly decorated white cake.

Lex merely smiles at me as he grabs a few strawberries and throws them into his mouth, vigorously chewing. "Feel free to grab whatever you like," he says.

I can't do anything but stare at the fantastic feast, saliva forming in my mouth, but to actually eat it? My eyes instantly drift toward Beast.

"Don't look at him," Lex commands

The rage in his eyes is almost too much to take, and when I pick up a knife and fork, all I want to do is stab him with it.

But if I did that, I'd never see the light of day again.

"Why did you invite me up here?" I ask.

"I'd like a little company while I eat," he responds. "After all, a man can get quite lonely when his wife goes off on a business trip."

He picks up another strawberry and chucks it in his mouth like no one's watching even though I can practically feel Beast's eyes penetrating my back.

"Go on. Eat." Lex stares me down until I finally pick up my fork and prick into an egg, placing it on my plate. He doesn't stop watching me until I've cut into it and taken a bite.

The taste is heavenly, so much more than I expected from my memories. It's been so long since I last tasted anything but stale bread, and it's making me tear up. Especially when I take one glance over my shoulder and see Beast lick his lips like he's picturing himself eating the same food.

The fork drops from my hand.

"What's wrong, dear?" Lex asks.

"This is wrong, and you know it," I reply.

He raises his brow, shoving a piece of bacon into his mouth. "What is?"

"Why are you feeding me but not him?"

He pauses and puts down his fork. "You sure sound like you care an awful lot."

My cheeks flush with heat, but I ignore it. "I want him to be able to eat just like us, that's all."

"Sure. The man who tried to kill you," he jests,

chuckling. "Needs food."

"*You* tried to kill me," I say. "It was *your* decision, not his."

He stops eating altogether now. "He is a tool. A pet. A dog. To do with as I please."

"He's a human being," I rebuke. "How can you treat someone like this?"

He slams his fist onto the table, and it makes me jolt up and down. "I will treat my dog anyway I damn well like!"

I swallow, the food I just ate feeling like it's making its way back up my throat. I feel guilty for even having taken a single bite.

"And you will eat when I tell you to. Now eat."

I stare at the plate, my hands shaking.

I feel the same way I did when he pushed me to scream out loud I was using Beast to get out. Like all of this … is a trap.

"Why?" I mutter. "Why now?"

"Hmm?" He looks up at me from his plate.

"All this time, you kept me in that cage, and now you suddenly treat me like a guest?" I don't trust this one bit.

"Did you forget you were the one who chose to go back down there instead of staying in my guest room?" he quips, licking his lips at me in a way that makes me feel like he wants to lick me instead, and my skin feels like it's crawling with bugs.

"No," I respond. "But why do you care so much if I eat? If I live at all?"

He laughs. "Oh girl, you really are stupid."

I'd be lying if I said that didn't sting.

"I am not—"

"You think I'd let you ruin *my* property?"

Property?

What?

"Why do you think your father owes me?" The sudden rage in his eyes catches me off guard.

"I don't know," I say.

He tilts his head. "He didn't let you in on his business, did he?"

I wonder where he's going with this. Why he invited me here to eat all this lavish food in this expensive dress. Why I'm being treated like a pretty doll on display.

"What do you want from me?" I ask.

"What do I want?" He takes another aggressive bite of his bacon. "You know what I want, girl. Money. And your father's head on my goddamn fork." He shoves it into his mouth like it's no big deal, while my stomach almost spins upside down.

"But you and that Beast have been getting in the way of what I want," Lex says.

"What?" I mutter, completely confused.

What does Beast have to do with this?

"You two have been getting along nicely, haven't you?" he adds.

It feels like all the blood is draining from my face.

"Even after you admitted you're only using him to get

out." The vicious smile on his face makes it impossible to breathe.

"No screaming, no slapping, no fighting, nothing …" he mutters, grabbing a piece of bread and taking a big bite. "I have to say, I'm a little disappointed."

"Stop," I hiss.

He chews and swallows. "Or what? What do you want to do, Aurora?" he muses, putting down the bread. "You wanna take a stab at me?"

"Don't tempt me," I say through gritted teeth.

He laughs gratuitously. "Oh, I love a little bit of sass."

He's making a joke out of me, and I hate it. I hate even being here in this dress, at this lavish table, with this man, in this freaking house. I just want to be free, but this guy won't let me.

"Be careful, girl. That kind of violence can come back to bite you," he says.

"Like it's come back to bite you?" I reply.

But the way he glares at me instantly makes me regret that decision.

"The only thing that's come back to bite me is my decision to loan money to your pig ass father all those years ago," he growls, spitting out pieces of bread. "Do you even know what it cost me?" He grabs a glass of water and chugs it down, spluttering half of it out as he adds, "My fucking company is on the brink. I need that money *now*."

I swallow back the shame. "Lending my papa money was your decision, not his. And I can't force him to give it to you."

He slams both hands on the table, making me scoot back in my seat. "It wasn't my choice to spend it all on surgeries to make *you* look normal!"

My pupils dilate, and I sit frozen in my chair.

It feels like the air has been forced out of my lungs.

What's been unspoken for years is now out in the open.

And every guard, every server, every person in this room heard.

Including Beast.

Time slows down as I turn my eyes away from this world, my ears ringing with the words he said. Words that strike me so hard my heart begins to palpitate. As sweat drops roll down my forehead, I clutch my chair.

And without thinking, I shove it back, running for the door as fast as I can.

Too late.

Not quick enough.

Two arms catch me halfway there, stopping me from exiting the room.

I panic and struggle against their grip.

"Where are you going?" Lex jests behind me. "Trying to leave now, when we've finally gotten to the good part?"

The guards grip me harshly while I look right at Beast and beg him with my eyes. "Please," I mutter.

And even though his eyes are riddled with pain, he doesn't budge as he stands near the wall like a stone giant, watching the whole scene unfold. His head tilts, the collar blinking in the lights. A stark reminder of his place in this world.

And mine, as the guards pull me away from him.

Lex marches toward me and forces me to look at him by grabbing my cheeks and pinching them. "Look at him." He turns my face to forcefully look into Beast's eyes, and the tears begin to roll down my face. "You haven't even told him, have you? Has he seen?"

Beast's face contorts as he watches us, his jaw clenched tight. And I wish, more than anything, I could cover his ears and eyes and stop him from hearing these words.

These words that rip through my soul.

"You're a Frankenstein," he growls.

And without a second thought, he grabs my arms by the elbow and rips off the gloves.

The small pieces of fabric protecting me from the harsh looks and judgment of the outside world.

The ones that kept people from looking at me like a freak. Like the monster I was born into.

Lex holds up my arms for all to see, the scars lining my skin, the deformed, crooked fingers … the missing ones.

Guards erupt into gasps and laughter, the same sounds I used to hear back in school.

Lex chucks the gloves on the floor right in front of Beast, the sound making me violently aware of how badly I wish I could hide myself from this world.

But there is no hiding from his perpetual gaze.

You're nothing. You're too ugly to look at. What are you doing here? You belong in a zoo.

All the things kids and adults said to me, floating through my head all at once.

But I can't look away.

Not from him.

The one beastly looking man who didn't see me that way because he didn't know.

And now … he does.

Twenty-Six

BEAST

Nothing could've prepared me for the amount of hatred that would fill my body the moment he tore off her gloves.

Not because of what she looks like, but because of how everyone else in this room reacted.

How my owner has turned her, the one girl who belongs to me, into an object of ridicule.

"All that fucking money, gone up into smoke to fix this." He flicks Aurora's wrist around, showing everyone the three fingers she has, which are thick and clubbed. "And it didn't even fucking work."

His words are like a knife, cutting deep into her. I can

see it from the way she looks at me, her eyes filling with more and more dread with every passing second.

And I wish I could take it all away.

He throws her arm down and clamps her chin between his fingers again and forces her to look at him. "You thought I didn't know what your father was up to all those years? What he spent *my* money on?"

Tears stream down her face as she shakes her head.

"What a fucking waste," he growls, and he directs her chin back toward me. "Look at her," my owner shouts at me. "Look at what you chose to bring home instead of kill. This monster is the reason you're still not free."

The reason I'm not free.

A monster.

Two words bound by one another.

Bound by rules, by injustice.

Just like us.

Aurora's eyes flicker with tears, but I refuse to look anywhere else, despite the fact that she's trying so desperately to look anywhere but at me. My owner won't let her.

"This is what you've been fucking around with," my owner tells me. "Was it worth it?"

"Stop," I say underneath my breath.

"What was that?" my owner barks, pointing at his ear. "I can't hear you with that goddamn collar around your neck."

He tilts his head and grabs one of her fingers and bends it until she screams. "Please!"

The mere thought of him hurting her pushes me over the edge.

Pushes me to rebel.

I take one step forward. But it's enough to make my owner stop midway through almost breaking her finger. A vicious smile forms on his face.

"So I was right. You have feelings for this girl, don't you?"

There's cruelty in his voice, but his words fade into nothingness when I look into her eyes. Because all I see is the same pain I've felt for years, reflected right back at me.

Shame. Neglect. Fear.

The kind that brings visceral pain.

All of it hiding under a thin veneer of a pretty face and a beautiful smile.

A smile I would break the world for.

"You actually fucked her, didn't you?" my owner asks with contempt.

When I nod, he begins to laugh.

"And you came inside that *thing*?"

Aurora's eyes beg me to make him stop, but I can't.

"Is it still dripping out of her?" he asks.

Some guards make obscene movements with their hips swaying back and forth, howling like actual wolves. I have no fucking clue what it means, but Aurora seems to get upset.

"Stop," she growls.

My owner, along with all his guards, continue laughing.

"And you let him?" he asks her.

"It was too late to stop," she murmurs with agony in her voice.

"Too late to stop, so now you might be pregnant," he mutters.

My owner shakes his head. "Well, if you won't get me his fucking money, maybe I can sell the fucking baby that spawns out of you in nine months."

Aurora's eyes widen in shock.

Does he mean … an actual baby?

Made because I spurted my seed inside her?

My jaw tightens.

Fuck. I never realized that was how humans were made. But it all makes sense when put together like that.

"Well, go on then. Show us how you used her," my owner suddenly says, laughing. "If it wasn't successful, let's make sure it is now."

He shoves her into my muscular chest so hard, her lungs empty into an *oompf* sound.

But when she looks up into my smoldering gaze and her eyes fill with tears, I want nothing more than to make everything around us disappear.

Everything … including him.

"Do it," my owner eggs me on, and he walks to the table and throws some of the food aside to make room. "Right there."

"What?" Aurora mutters.

"You heard me," my owner muses. "If you're gonna use

him, then do it right. Give me something I can work with. Maybe your darling *papa* will finally come to pick you up if he realizes how high the stakes are."

Aurora looks mortified as Raymond steps forward and grabs her arm, tearing her away from me. He hauls her to the table and shoves her against it. "Stay there," he spits, and he releases her, only to wipe his own hands like he thinks touching her will make him dirty.

And it makes me want to tear his head off his body.

"Fuck him," my owner says. "Fuck him like you mean it and show your *papa* how bad he screwed up."

She swallows, visibly shaking. "You can't be serious."

"I'm dead serious," he replies.

"But that's blackmail," she says.

"If it gets me my money," my owner says, shrugging. "You threw yourself at him so easily before. Now show me what you're willing to do to get out of that goddamn cell."

Raymond walks up to me and eyes me down before gazing at Aurora like she's some piece of meat he still wants to eat. "Be a good boy and fuck that girl while we watch."

I stay put, staring Aurora down, wishing she could see into my mind. Because if she could, she'd know the last thing I want to do is hurt her.

"Do it!" my owner barks.

With my head held high, I growl back, "No."

A sudden electrical jolt to my neck has me grunting. My fingers immediately claw at my neck, the pain immeasurable. I roar out loud, trying my best to stay standing, even though all the muscles in my body are contracting.

"Stop!" Aurora begs. "Please!"

When it finally ends, my eyes find her first.

Her.

It's always been about her.

Every inch of my struggles, all culminating in this one moment.

And when she nods, it's all I need to breathe.

"I'll do it," she mutters, the last tear rolling down her cheek.

But all I see is the woman who stopped my pain from consuming me whole.

Pain I'm now forced to give to her.

"You heard her, Beast. Fuck her then," my owner barks.

My heart bleeds as I haul myself forward, each of my steps heavier than the ones before. The closer I get, the more my heart comes back alive, the room feeling smaller and more intimate than I remember the second I'm right in front of her.

If I don't do this, neither of us will make it out alive.

But her eyes … they lure me in and tell me it's okay as I plant my hands beside her and lean in to whisper into her ear. "I don't want to hurt you … I want you to be free."

She sucks in a breath, and when I look at her, she seems genuinely surprised.

"I-I …" she murmurs.

But I place a finger on her lips. "They can hear," I whisper.

She nods softly, her lips parting as my finger draws down, my eyes mesmerized by her beauty. All this time, I thought she was hiding from me because she was scared, because she feared my scars, my violence. But now, I see the naked truth beneath these layers of protection she placed around her heart.

She was hiding her own body from the world. From me.

Just because her father told her to. Because this man, my owner, lent all the money to her father just so he could try to change her into something she's not.

I grab her arm and slide my hand down until I touch her skin right where her glove used to be. My fingers slowly slide down her scars and malformed bones, taking in what she looks like while keeping my gaze on her eyes. I don't need to see to know. I can feel my way across.

And when I reach the tip of her fingers, I bring them to my lips, kissing each one.

Her face burns bright with hope.

And I lean in and press a gentle kiss onto her lips, not wanting to scare her away. She's frozen in place, but her lips still move with mine, coaxing me, drawing out my tongue.

I lift her from the floor and set her down on the table between all the plates and food. It smells delicious, and the thought of having a bite screws with my head. But none of it could ever compare to claiming her.

So I dive right back in to kissing her, licking the roof of her mouth like it's the final chance I'll get at kissing her.

The guards behind us snigger, but I ignore their

presence and focus on her and her alone, kissing her like no one is watching.

"I'm scared," she whispers between kisses.

"Do you want to do this?" I ask, planting a kiss on her chin. When she nods, I let my lips roam freely across her neck. "I'll protect you."

She nods again and closes her eyes as I wrap my arm around her back and position myself between her legs. Her shoes clamp around my ass as she reels me in, trying to shield herself from the men's gazes while I pull down her panties underneath her dress.

My fingers slide up and down her thighs until I reach that sweet spot that makes her suck in a breath.

And all the men in the room chuckle.

Her body shivers, and she struggles to stay put as her hands are behind her back. She refuses to bring them to the side to support her body, but I understand why.

Everyone is watching her.

Judging her.

Laughing at her.

"Don't pay attention to them," I whisper as I look into her eyes. "Focus on me."

She doesn't look away as I start rolling my fingers around her pussy, focusing specifically on her clit until she's wet enough for me to enter.

And I push down my pants far enough until I can pull out my cock.

Gasps erupt from the guards when they see my size, but

I don't bother looking at them as I push up her dress far enough for me to get close without them seeing a single inch of her skin.

The tip of my dick is right up against her entrance. "Are you ready?"

She swallows, her skin glowing red with embarrassment.

"Don't give them anything," I whisper as I inch closer and closer, narrowing the gap between us until I finally enter her. "No gaze, no sigh, no moan. Nothing." Right then, I plunge in, and when her lips form an o-shape, I cover her mouth with mine, swallowing her sounds.

I fuck her fast and deep, burying myself to the hilt each time I do, not wanting to waste a single second of what might be my last chance to ever make love to her.

I never once used to care about anything but myself and my own life until I stepped into her home and laid eyes on her. That was the moment I knew … that girl was going to change me forever.

And when I kiss her, I kiss her with everything I have left to give.

"Look at them go!" one of the guards yelps, while another one whistles with both fingers.

But all I hear are her heady breaths and all the moans she swallows as I pound into her pussy. I can't look anywhere else but right into her eyes, not wanting to miss a single second of her unraveling as she clenches her legs tighter and tighter, her breathing growing more rapid with every thrust.

When her eyes close, I groan, "Look at me." Her eyes burst open at my command, and it riles me up to no end. "Eyes on me when you come. No one else. Only me."

With flushed cheeks, she nods, looking more and more delirious with every thrust I give her. Her pussy feels so tight and wet around my shaft, and I can barely contain myself. But I want to feel her fall apart first before I let myself go.

I lean into her and press a kiss to her lips. "Does it feel good?"

She bites her lip and nods, which is enough for me, as I plow into her until her eyes almost roll into the back of her head. But her eyes still manage to find the men behind me.

So I claim her attention by sinking my teeth into her shoulder.

She gasps in shock, and whispers, "Oh God …"

"Focus on the pain," I groan against her skin, fucking her while biting her until she no longer looks at them. Until my teeth are sunken into her flesh so deep they leave a bloodied mark.

And then I feel her pussy contract around my cock.

Before even a single moan rolls off her tongue, I pull away from her shoulder and cover her mouth with mine, stealing every single sound she makes until her orgasm finishes.

All of it belongs to me and only me.

When she's finished, I pull out my dick and slide my length across her pussy underneath her dress until I explode. Grinding my teeth to stop the groan from spilling out, I spread my juices all over. When my dick deflates, I pull away and tuck it back into my pants.

Her eyes scatter in the light as mine travel across her skin and the mark I left. A droplet of blood rolls down her shoulder, but I pick it up before it has a chance to land on her dress and bring it to my mouth, licking it up. The taste is exquisite, nothing like I could ever imagine.

With my eyes on her, I go to my knees in front of her and lift her panties all the way, sealing my cum inside. No one in this room saw even an inch of her skin, except for me.

So none of them will ever find out I didn't obey my owner's orders.

"Well, that was anticlimactic," one of the guards sputters.

"Yeah, we didn't even see any of the action," another guard spouts. "He blocked the view."

My owner smacks one of them against the arms and laughs. "You horny bastards."

They all laugh, but my attention is on her and her alone. "Are you okay?"

She nods, but she begins to blush even more, as though she's embarrassed we did this. "You … bit me," she murmurs, and her eyes go over the mark.

"To keep you from seeing them," I say as I caress her cheek.

She leans into the palm of my hand. "We did what Lex wanted. Now those guards won't hurt you anymore."

Her words make my heart thrum.

"I just want us both to be free," she adds.

I swallow. Even now, after what I did with her, she still thinks of me and what I need.

She grabs a piece of bread from the table and holds it in front of my mouth until my lips part and the food slides in. I haven't had bread in years, but the taste is amazing.

"Hey, no eating!" a guard interrupts, and he whips out his stun gun.

I quickly chuck the bread back onto her plate. Even though she meant well, it's not allowed, and I'm not about to risk it all over a piece of bread.

"What the …?" my owner growls, his eyes flicking from me to Aurora. "You actually liked doing that?"

He suddenly marches at Raymond and snatches the button that controls my collar out of his hand. With rage in his eyes, he presses the button so wildly, it instantly knocks me off balance and down onto the floor.

"No, stop it!" Aurora yells as I roar in pain.

"You don't get to enjoy that, you beast!" my owner barks at me.

The pain is too intense to even speak.

"Please, stop," Aurora begs.

I've never heard someone beg for my life. Never.

And it's the only thing that keeps me from roaring out in agony.

Only after multiple pleas does the zapping finally pause. I breathe out ragged breaths, my heart going a million miles an hour as I wait out the muscle cramps.

"That should teach you," my owner growls. His phone suddenly rings and he picks it up, shouting into the mic. "What?!"

My eyes instinctively draw toward the conversation. Something doesn't feel right.

"Good. Someone finally did their fucking job," Lex shouts, and he flicks his fingers at Raymond. "Get the car."

What's going on?

"Yes, sir," the guard responds, and one of them runs off, leaving us all in this room with two guards, one of who has twitchy fingers as he clutches the stun gun.

"Take him," my owner commands, and the guards hoist me off the floor and drag me away before I can even say another word to Aurora, even though she looks at me in misery.

"Where are you taking him?" she asks, as she hops off the table and pats down her dress.

Lex flicks his fingers at a guard stationed outside the door, and before I'm pushed out, I can still hear him say, "Bring her too. We're going to see your precious *papa*."

Twenty-Seven

Aurora

Papa?
They found him?
Oh God. How?

Panic floods my veins, but I can't even respond before the guard hauls me away through the same door they just took Beast through.

"Let go of me!" I screech as the guy drags me through the hallway and into a garage where maybe a dozen cars are neatly lined, along with that familiar van, of which the engine is already warming up.

The van door opens and Raymond's face appearing from behind it makes all the blood leave my face as I'm shoved inside.

"Welcome back, little monster," he says as he grasps my wrists and ties them together with a tie wrap. "You know, I'm starting to miss those gloves."

I spit in his face.

The payback is swift and painful.

SMACK!

My head is tilted from the strike to my cheek.

"And don't try that shit on me again, or I'll fucking hit you where it really hurts," he growls, tightening the wraps even more.

"Where's Beast?" I ask.

He laughs. "Why do you care?" He raises his brows. "Aw, you growing attached to that fucker after he gave you a little dicking?"

"He's more of a man than you'll ever be," I quip. I'm normally never this brazen, but I can't sit idly by anymore when my whole world is being turned upside down.

"Shut up," Raymond growls back, and he stuffs a piece of cloth in my mouth. "I've heard enough from you."

A hood is pulled over my head and secured tightly behind my neck.

I feel like I can't breathe.

Within seconds, the van begins to drive.

Oh God. I can't believe this is really happening.

Where are they keeping Beast?

Why isn't he here in this van with me?

All I can think about is how much pain he must be in

after getting zapped in the neck not once but twice. All for trying to protect me.

The guard keeps a watchful gaze on me, his hand on his gun at all times. There's nothing I can do but sit and wait until we arrive. If I try anything, he'll surely shoot me.

If they've found my father … there's no reason for me to still be alive.

I gulp down the fear and focus on the sounds around me, the engine running, the wheels turning, the gravel underneath as we drive off. I focus on the road, the turns we make, and the sounds of the people and traffic outside.

It feels like an eternity has passed before the van finally stops.

A hand wraps around my arm and tugs me along violently, shoving me out of the van, before tearing the hood off my face.

I gasp in the oxygen while looking around.

We're at a big warehouse near the docks. There's a ton of noise all around us from ships and crew toiling about, large structures all around us, and my eyes can't stop taking it all in.

Another car stops near the building, and Lex and a couple of his guards along with Beast step out of the vehicle. My heart skips a beat the moment our eyes connect.

"Move." A guard pushes me so hard I almost fall down.

"Hey!" Beast growls at him.

"What?!" The guard barks back.

Lex looks at Beast with disdain, and he points at his

pocket. "Remember who owns you."

Beast's nostrils flare, but he stays put, despite his muscles being tenser than before. I know he wants to help, but I don't want to see him in pain either.

I swallow and walk forward to where the guard guides me, through the giant doors and into the warehouse. The place is barely lit, even though the sun is going down, and I have to open my eyes wide to see anything at all.

There are several rooms in the building, all stacked to the ceiling with boxes full of goods. Packages, marihuana, white powder, guns.

I swallow at the sight of so many illicit goods, wondering where the hell we are.

I'm shoved into a big room in the back, where there's a desk and a computer, along with a couch and a bookcase filled with paper. An office.

"HMRR!?"

The sound of my father's voice makes me turn my head.

He's right there, on the other side of the office, strapped to a chair with a piece of cloth in his mouth.

"Papa!" I scream, and my muscles flinch as I try to run, but another guard stops me before my first step is taken.

Is this where he's been hiding all this time? A warehouse?

Lex and all his guards as well as Beast come into the office too, and they all stand around him like it's one big show and we're the audience.

"Well, well, well … if it isn't the fucking coward Blom," Lex says, laughing out loud. "Finally found you, rat!" Lex circles him. "Not so pompous now, are we?"

Father keeps looking at me with bloodshed, teary eyes like I need to … save him.

His whole body is shaking, and there's blood dripping down his forehead and legs.

They hurt him.

"Let him go," I yell. "He needs medical attention."

Lex pauses in his tracks and laughs. "You think I'd let him go? After searching for him for so long?" He shakes his finger at me. "You're messing with the wrong guy, little girl."

"GHMRRR!" my father screeches through the cloth again.

I wish I could take it off. I wish I could take all of the ropes around his body off and help him on his feet, so we could run away together. But a guard's hands squeezing the blood out of my arm remind me what little power I have.

Lex grabs my father by the hair, tilting his head. "You thought we wouldn't catch you?" He smacks my father right across the face. "I *always* get what I want."

He smears some of the blood on my father's clothes. "I'm so glad at least one of my guards was able to track you down." Now he raises his eyes at Beast, and the intent glare doesn't go unnoticed.

"So what have we learned from all of this?" Lex muses as he circles my father. "That you cannot be trusted with even a dollar of my fucking money." He pauses and clenches my father's shoulders. "You used all of my money on that *monster*."

He points at me, and it feels like the earth is caving in underneath my feet.

Tears stain my eyes as my fingers dig into my skin.

"And you know, I wouldn't even mind, if you'd paid me back," Lex continues. "But you didn't. No, you had to go and lie your way through everything. Cheat me out of my hard-earned money. Just so you could steal it all and run away with it," he growls, his grip on my father's shoulders intensifying. "All this …" He looks around the office and into the warehouse. "And for what? Hmm? It wasn't for her, that's for sure."

The way he looks at me makes me want to cry.

Lex flicks his fingers, and all the guards suddenly walk toward my father.

Oh God.

Are they going to kill him?

"No, please, don't hurt him!" I shriek.

They pick up his chair and haul him out of the office.

Lex walks past me but pauses to whisper into my ear, "Are you sure you should be worried about his life when yours is no longer of value to me?"

My stomach almost turns upside down right then, and I have to physically swallow down the bile.

"Come and witness your father's demise," he says, squeezing my shoulder, "and maybe, just maybe …"

He doesn't finish his sentence. Instead, he walks right past me into the main hall, where they've left my father on his chair. He's rocking about, desperately trying to free himself, to no avail.

All it does is make the guards, and Lex, laugh.

The only ones who aren't laughing are Beast and me.

Lex circles my father again and grabs him by the throat. "Well, c'mon then, explain to your daughter what the fuck you've been up to."

He rips the piece of cloth out of my father's mouth.

"This is just a warehouse. None of it is—"

WHACK!

Lex smacks him across the face. "Don't. Lie."

"All right, all right, yes, I used this warehouse to trade around some stuff. It was only so I could make the money back," my father explains.

"Money you owed me," Lex adds.

"Yes, yes, but I promise, I can pay you back now," he says, his eyes drifting to a particular box in the back. "There's money in there. Enough to pay off everything I owe."

Lex smiles and leans in. "You think I'd be satisfied with a little payment?" He fishes a knife from his pocket and rams it straight into Papa's thigh.

I gasp in shock as my father screams out in pain and begins to cry.

"Please! Please, have mercy. I'll give you everything I have," my father begs.

"ENOUGH!" Lex pulls his knife from my father's leg and cleans it on his shirt. "You've had enough time. I gave you a chance to pay me back, over and over again. And now I've finally had enough."

"What do you want? I'll give you anything," my father says. "You want more than just money? I have plenty stacked in boxes. You can take all my heroin and cocaine. Take the weed and the guns. I don't care. You can have it all. It's yours."

I hate seeing him like this. I hate what his business has done to him. What his business has done to us.

"No amount of money will give me back the trust and patience I lost, Blom," Lex growls. "No more negotiations. You had your shot. So now, I'll take *all* of your money and destroy you."

I shake my head. "Please, don't kill him."

Lex glares at me now, and it feels like I'm being choked by nothing but thin air. "Why do you think I brought you here, Aurora?"

I'm too stunned to speak.

"ANSWER ME!"

"I don't know. To let me free?"

He laughs maniacally but it suddenly ends. "No." His smile is gone. "To let you watch the man who spent *my* money on you die."

The guard shoves a gun into Beast's hand. My jaw drops but he seems as surprised as I am.

"And my dog will do it for me," he growls.

My eyes widen. I shake my head, tears streaming down my face. "Please, no. Don't do this."

But Lex completely ignores me as he focuses on Beast, who just stands there with the gun in his hand. "Now prove your loyalty to me, Beast. And maybe I will finally release you from your chains and give you what you always wanted …" Beast's eyes flicker with promise as they home in on Lex as he mutters the word, "Freedom."

Twenty-Eight

BEAST

Freedom.

The moment he says the word out loud, everything around me ceases to exist.

Years. Years of my life spent in captivity. In solitude.

All because I was taken off the streets and turned into a fighting machine to please whatever man would call himself my owner.

Could it all come to an end today?

The mere thought makes me acutely aware of the gun that's pressed into my hand, and I look down to stare at it, to feel the weight of it shift between my fingers.

"Kill him," my owner says through gritted teeth.

"No!" Aurora screams, but I barely register it.

All I can focus on is that one word.

The word that was promised to me if I did as I was told and completed all my tasks.

Freedom. Freedom. Freedom.

The only thing I've wanted. The only thing I've craved for so many goddamn years.

Right within my fingertips.

"Go on then," the guard growls at me.

Instinctively, my feet move toward the guy in the chair. His face is sweaty, and his thick body is covered in blood. He's muttering words I don't understand, but he panics once I'm in front of him and place the gun to his head.

"You don't have to do this, boy. You can still be free. If you help me, I'll help you," he says in an erratic tone.

"Please, don't do this, Beast," Aurora's voice makes me turn my head. "He's the only family I have left. Don't take him from me."

Her words make it harder and harder to shove the gun into his head.

But I have to. If I don't, my owner will hurt me. And I will never be given the freedom I so desperately crave.

"Shut up, girl!" the guard growls at her, and he puts a hand over her mouth.

"Pwease!" Aurora still mumbles through his hand.

"Ignore her, Beast," my owner says as he hovers close by, his voice laced with poison. "Do what you were born to do. Kill."

Kill. Kill. Kill.

Everything I've ever known.

All that's ever mattered.

Until … her.

My head still turns as I look at the girl I once thought was a nuisance, a sidestep in my mission. The pain in her eyes causes such a visceral reaction in my body that I struggle to even breathe.

"You want her?" Blom suddenly says, drawing my attention back to him. "You can have her if you save me."

"Shut up, you fucking fool," my owner spits. "Do it. Kill him now, Beast!"

But my eyes are glued to Blom as I push the safety off the gun.

Time seems to last an infinity right now as I'm faced with my options.

Kill for freedom and destroy her forever.

Or …

"She's yours, I swear," Blom splutters, droplets of blood spilling from his mouth as he speaks. "I don't even want her. I never did."

His words make my eyes widen and my heart pulse in my throat.

"All my problems are because of her," he says through gritted teeth. "She killed my wife, the only woman I ever loved, just by being born. She's a monster."

***

Aurora

What?

I blink through the tears, staring at my father, wondering if I really heard that.

I don't even want her. I never did.

His words repeat over and over again in my head like a never-ending stream of hatred all directed at me.

I killed his wife.

My mother.

Just by being born.

I've always known it was my fault. I got stuck inside her and she bled to death.

Never once have I stopped feeling guilty because of it.

But I thought Papa loved me, and that pulled me through all these years.

Until now.

Until he uttered those words.

I don't even want her. I never did.

She's a monster.

"Papa," I murmur, my voice tiny like that of a bug.

My heart feels like it's been ripped out of my chest and stomped on.

Like I've been cast aside.

Made worthless.

Like the monster I was born into.

"What? Don't act like you didn't know," my father shouts, his face all red. "Pretending to be all happy with those gloves."

I stare at my hands, at the three deformed fingers, remembering how dutifully I covered them each and every time I went anywhere outside because he told me to. Because he made me promise to wear those gloves.

More tears form in my eyes. I shake my head, not wanting to face my own destruction, but a guard holds me back from turning around. All eyes are on me. Even my father's, whose eyes show no mercy. Not a single ounce.

Beast's gun pushes into my father's forehead, his face contorting. "You …"

My father closes his eyes, scrunching up his face like he's expecting the bullet any second now. But I only feel numb to the core.

***

BEAST

This motherfucker dared to tell me, to tell her, that she wasn't wanted.

I've never wanted to kill a man more in my life.

My fingers push against the trigger, desperate to pull it.

One shot, that's all I'd need. One shot to end it all.

End my captivity.

End her suffering.

I swallow and gaze at her over my shoulder, but the tears running down her cheeks and the distraught look on her face still catch me off guard. I never expected I'd grow to care so much about another human being.

He broke her.

With a few words, he managed to do what not even my owner was capable of.

All the shine, all the hope, all the love for life, erased in a few seconds.

All because of this fucker.

This fucker who is her father. Her papa. The one person she never stopped caring about. The one she wanted to protect at all cost. The only family she has left.

"You don't deserve her," I mutter under my breath.

His eyes widen.

"Yes, kill him," my owner growls from behind me, and he steps away.

My teeth grind into each other.

I thought I knew who I was. What I wanted. What I needed.

But when our eyes connect again, I finally know for sure.

This girl … I would sacrifice it all for her.

"No."

I turn around and aim my gun at the men behind me, at

the guard who holds her down.

BANG!

The bullet enters his skull, and he drops onto the floor, blood pouring from the wound.

Everyone looks shocked, but my eyes are only on Aurora as I want her to know the truth. Everyone here is a monster … except her.

And without looking away, I aim my gun at my owner and shoot.

But the gun doesn't go off.

I shoot again and again, but the clip is empty.

Guards all around us pull their guns and point them at me.

Fuck.

My owner looks livid. "Motherfu—You dare to shoot down my own men?"

He stomps toward me and presses the button so harshly that I collapse onto the ground immediately, the electrical current running through my body too strong to take.

"You had one job," my owner growls. "One bullet, and you wasted it on my guard instead of that fucker?!"

The electricity makes me curl up into a ball, and the empty gun drops from my hand.

"What a disappointment. You deserve every ounce of pain," my owner growls while my muscles contort. "Why? Why would you not just shoot that asshole? *He* deserved it!"

My eyes almost feel like they're about to pop out of my skull. It hurts so much I can't breathe. But I still manage to answer. "Because she *loves* him."

I look up into her eyes, those magnificent eyes that dared to look at me like a normal human being, even when no one else would.

"You fucking betrayed me!" my owner yells, and he applies another jolt so powerful it twists my stomach. But when I look at her, every second of pain is worth it.

Her lips part, her face twisted with emotions, but nonetheless beautiful. A perfect picture for my last day on this earth. And when my eyes close, I take the pain and disappear into myself.

"Beast!" Aurora's voice keeps me afloat, keeps me here, in the now. "Don't give up! Fight!"

My eyes burst open, only to watch my owner stomp to one of his guards and snatch his gun from his hands. "I'll finish this myself."

And he marches right over to her father with the gun aimed at his head.

Even though the zaps are still burning up my body, I push myself up from the concrete floor before he can get there, finding the energy in her voice alone.

With all of my leftover strength, I push my fingers between the collar and pull as hard as I have ever pulled until the metal comes apart at the screws. I roar as the material bends and twists out of shape far enough for me to rip it apart.

I chuck it onto the floor.
CLING CLANG!

All the guards focus on the metal. Then their gazes swoop up to meet mine.

And as my owner stands in front of the one man who deserves death, I grab his wrist and push him away before he pulls the trigger.

BANG!

The bullet ricochets across the walls of the warehouse.

But there has never been a stronger silence than there is now.

"You …" My owner grits, his eyes widening at the sight of my missing collar. "How di—"

I punch him in the face as hard as I can. He falls back on his ass, blood pouring from his nose.

The guards scream out in vigor, pulling out their guns, waiting only on their boss's signal.

But all I care about is saving her.

Aurora suddenly bolts toward me, emblazoned by the same courage that burst through my veins moments ago.

She hides behind me, and I shield her with my body as I hand her my knife. Without a second thought, she cuts her father loose, even with her tied-up hands. He doesn't say thanks or even look at her before he runs off toward the exit.

"SHOOT HIM!" my owner roars.

And the explosion of bullets begins.

BANG! BANG! BANG!

There is only one thing on my mind.

The end.

But it *cannot* be hers.

I once told those guards if they hurt her, I'd eat them alive.

Time to make good on that promise.

Twenty-Nine

Aurora

Time's up.

One second, I look at my father running away, and the next, the entire room fills with smoke and gunfire.

Everything happens so fast that it doesn't even register, but I can't close my eyes.

Because Beast has finally been unchained.

He grabs the chair and turns the seat up, using it and his body as a shield to protect me from the bullets. His roars go through marrow and bone as bullets enter his thigh and arms, but his strength doesn't wane one bit.

When the gunfire momentarily stops, he throws the

chair into the guards and unleashes his wrath.

He runs at them at full speed like a bull, ramming into one of them, only to pick him up and throw him into another guard like a bowling ball into a pin. He spins on his heels, grabs a guard's wrist with a gun pointed at his head, and twists the man's hand until it breaks.

The guard cries out in pain, but Beast turns the gun until it's aimed at the guard's face.

BANG!

Another one drops onto the floor.

BANG, BANG!

Shots follow Beast around as he runs from side to side, knocking everyone down with ease. Shrieks are audible all around as I duck and hide near the ground while he goes on a streak.

One guard is grabbed by the collar and put right into the aim of an incoming bullet, ravaging his heart. Beast chucks aside his body and storms at the guy who shot, ripping his legs from underneath his body, cracking them in two places until he screams and begs for mercy.

"No, no, please, stop!"

Beast ignores every single one of his pleas and stomps on his face until it cracks his skull.

Another one runs at him with a big butcher knife. Beast stands up, his eyes almost unrecognizable, filled with fire and a hunger for blood.

A hunger he's about to satiate.

Another guard attacks him, but instead of hitting him,

Beast grabs him, pulls him close, and takes an actual bite out of his neck. Blood sprays everywhere as he casts aside a chunk of flesh, and the guard stumbles away, shrieking his lungs out as he clutches his neck.

"You'll pay for that!" Raymond growls at him as he dodges a bullet.

But the moment Raymond runs at Beast, he simply rams him into the ground, grabs his legs, and splits them open like a rip at the seam until they're dislodged. Raymond cries out in pain, but the sounds end as quickly as they came when Beast buries his knife in his throat and slices him open from left to right.

More guards run at him, but they're no match for him.

The collar around his neck kept him on a leash and made it easy to control him.

But now that it's off, all the pain and suffering are coming full circle.

And vengeance becomes him.

His roars are like fuel to his might as he chucks one of his knives at a guard's throat, making blood squirt out. A kick to the stomach has another one of the guards barfing, and Beast simply rips out his tongue and pulls out his eyes like it comes effortlessly.

And I'm completely blown away by the sheer display of power.

Like a walking, living god, he wreaks havoc on anyone and everyone who gets in his way.

Bullets graze and hit him, but it's like he doesn't even

care. Like his body is made of pure fury and ruin as he fights his way through each and every one of the guards until only a few are left.

"BEAST!" Lex roars with rage.

Avoiding the gunfire by crawling across the floor, Lex reaches the gun Beast knocked from his hand and points it right at him.

And I don't know what comes over me, but I rush to him and shove his hand to the side right before he pulls the trigger.

BANG!

The bullet grazes my cheek, the pain instant, sizzling.

I fall away from him, and as he comes to a stand, he points the gun right at my face.

"NO!" The visceral pain in Beast's voice as it blasts across the warehouse instantly draws my attention. He punches one of the guards in the jaw so hard it dislocates, and he rushes toward me.

Lex's eyes widen as he spots him, and he immediately withdraws and screams at his guards, "Shoot him! NOW!"

BANG!

The bullet hits his back right as he stops in front of me, and his body caves to the multiple wounds. On hands and knees, he comes to me.

"He hurt you," he murmurs with blood on his lips. He reaches for the wound on my face, but he collapses before he manages to touch me. Tears well up in my eyes.

"Beast," I mutter, crawling closer to grab his shoulders.

"Please, I don't want you to die."

But I can't help him get up. I'm a bug compared to him. How could I possibly help?

His bloodied hand fumbles near his pocket, but he still manages to fish out something.

A dried-up pink flower.

The same kind of flowers that used to grow in the garden outside my house.

The flowers I often picked as a child.

"You asked me why …" he says, and he pushes the dried flower into my hand. "*This* is why."

I thought I'd cried all the tears I had left to cry.

But I was wrong.

So wrong.

Because when I look at this flower, everything I ever thought about him begins to unravel like a string being pulled apart.

I remember this flower and the day I gave it away like it was yesterday.

Time feels like it ceases to exist. At this moment, all I can do is look into his soul-shattering eyes, wondering how I didn't see before.

"It's you," I mutter, tears rolling down my cheeks. "You're the boy in the bathroom."

The boy in the bathroom who escaped and lived on the streets for years … all thanks to my father. The same man he just saved from certain death.

"You remember," he mutters.

"You knew it was me?" I reply, tears rolling freely down my cheeks.

He nods.

All these years, he kept this flower that I gave him.

I look at the flower. "How is this possible?" is all I can muster.

But then my mind remembers all the moments he was facing the wall, all the shuffling and rummaging. He must've kept it in his cell, behind a stone.

I smile at the idea, but my smile instantly fades the second I realize all the time we had is spent.

Lex laughs maniacally. "All this strength wasted on a simple girl and her idiot father," he muses. "What a waste."

He points his gun at Beast, but Beast simply looks at me and says, "Run."

One second.

That's all it takes for me to accept what he's giving me.

A final chance at freedom.

The one thing he's fought for all his life.

I run as fast as I can, bolting for the same exit my father ran through.

Behind me, more shouting ensues, and when I look back, a guard has his gun aimed at my back.

Beast leans up with what final strength he still has in his bones and throws a knife at the man, knocking him down.

"You fucking bastard!" Lex growls at him.

But I never stop running.

Not because I don't want to.

I desperately do.

But because he told me to.

Because I know the value of his gift to me.

And when I take one final glance over my shoulder and see Lex standing over Beast's body with a gun aimed at him, I hold my breath.

BANG!

THANK YOU

FOR READING!

Thank you so much for reading BEAST. Make sure to pick up BEAUTY as well! Now available on Amazon.

You can also stay up to date of new books via my website: www.clarissawild.com

I'd love to talk to you! You can find me on Facebook: www.facebook.com/ClarissaWildAuthor, make sure to click LIKE.

You can also join the Fan Club: www.facebook.com/groups/FanClubClarissaWild and talk with other readers!

Enjoyed this book? You could really help out by leaving a review on Amazon and Goodreads. Thank you!

ALSO BY CLARISSA WILD

Dark Romance
Debts & Vengeance Series
Dellucci Mafia Duet
The Debt Duet
Savage Men Series
Delirious Series
Indecent Games Series
The Company Series
FATHER

New Adult Romance
Fierce Series
Blissful Series
Ruin
Rowdy Boy & Cruel Boy

Erotic Romance
The Billionaire's Bet Series
Enflamed Series
Unprofessional Bad Boys Series

Visit Clarissa Wild's website for current titles.
www.clarissawild.com

ABOUT THE AUTHOR

Clarissa Wild is a New York Times & USA Today Bestselling author of Dark Romance and Contemporary Romance novels. She is an avid reader and writer of swoony stories about dangerous men and feisty women. Her other loves include her hilarious husband, her cutie pie son, her two crazy but cute dogs, and her ninja cat that sometimes thinks he's a dog too. In her free time, she enjoys watching all sorts of movies, playing video games, reading tons of books, and cooking her favorite meals.

Want to be informed of new releases and special offers? Sign up for Clarissa Wild's newsletter on her website www.clarissawild.com.

Visit Clarissa Wild on Amazon for current titles.

Printed in Great Britain
by Amazon